THE GAME

ALEX BOS

For my grandparents.

Thank you for braving the *rimboe*.

"Reality is an acquired taste."

- Matthew Perry

CHAPTER ONE

Strike 3

I think the most intimate thing you can show a person is your bare mattress. I'd rather show a man my naked body. Showered, of course. Plucked, shaved and waxed. Tanned if possible.

My mattress is the old-fashioned kind, floral and satin, with twenty years of gentle staining.

I inherited it from my parents. Which makes the fact that I'm sleeping on its bare surface even worse.

The newest stain is cream concealer, the drugstore brand. I peel the false eyelashes from my eyelids and set them on the floor beside me.

It's 11:45 a.m.

I don't have to go to the bathroom–a bad sign. Am I hungover? Probably. But what kind?

Will it be a sick-to-my-stomach wine hangover? Or a bloated, acrid, biting cheap-beer-hangover?

I sit up, a little too fast. The nausea is overwhelming. The blood vessels in my head throb, emptied too quickly.

There's a pile of clean laundry next to me on the bed. I push it to the side and lay back down, carefully placing my left cheek back onto the concealer stain, lest I create a new one.

It's 12:45. It's 1:24. It's 2:02. It's 2:03.

I consider checking my phone. What if someone needs me?

What if no one does?

Which is worse?

Six missed calls.

Mom.

Mom.

Mom.

Mom.

Mom.

Mom.

A sharp, irate knock on the door jogs my memory. She's here for community service. We're going to community service.

Court-ordered community service.

I feel the tightness of anger in my chest and it reminds me that as long as I live and breathe, I'm going to have to face this shit.

Honestly, I'd rather die. But only if dying was easy, instant, and required no forethought or planning.

A second, even more irate knock is followed by Debbie's shrill voice.

"Time to go, Lyss," she says.

I take a make-up wipe to my face, walk to the bathroom, look in the mirror. Not bad.

Not good. But honestly, not bad, all things considered.

I do not moisturize. I *do* brush my teeth.

I walk into the kitchen wearing the same clothes I slept in last night, and confirm that the culprit of my headache (and in fact, all my woes) is indeed a box of Redvolution on the counter.

I pick it up to assess the damage.

Empty.

But at least the bag is still in the box, which I stash under the sink.

I open the door to my apartment. My mother is flustered, but this is also her default, so I don't take it personally or even very seriously.

"Gonna be late," she says, peering around the kitchen. "God, Alyssa. Could you have managed to clean up a little? Not like you have anything else to do."

I roll my eyes. "I'm doing it today. After. I always clean on Saturdays–you know that."

This whole string of words is a frantic lie. I know it. She knows it. But neither of us is ready for *that* fight.

"Well I can tell you one thing," she persists, "It's *not* going to be like this when you move in."

We walk out the front door. The air is cool and fresh and moist—it's spring air. For a very short moment, I forget my life is in shambles and anticipate the heat of summer.

"Your father and I spoke about it this morning," my mother starts the car, "and we have agreed that we need to set some boundaries. It's not going to be a free-for-all."

I place my forehead on the window. The coolness of the glass provides instant relief for my throbbing head.

"I know," I say.

"Your father wants you to pay rent," she takes a bite of a fast food sandwich, "but I told him you couldn't afford it."

My mother pauses. She looks over at me, waiting for me to thank her.

"Thank you," I oblige.

It's not the thanks she was looking for. Take two.

I try again, "That was really kind of you Mom. I appreciate it. You didn't have to do that."

If she were directing a play about my life, she'd ask me to run that line again, this time with a little more feeling.

"Say it like you know how disappointed she is in you. You're her only daughter, and now you have to move back in. At thirty. Say it like you know how much you owe her," she'd say.

Or maybe she'd just go back to Act I, Scene I and make me–better.

Instead, she says, "I hope Darren doesn't mind that you're dressed like that."

Darren is a "connection" of my mother's. I think they met at the food pantry.

"You're lucky you're not picking up trash on the side of the road," she turns into an unmarked parking lot.

"Thank you for the ride," I grab my bag. "He knows I'm coming today, right?"

"Yes Alyssa, he knows you're coming. I'll see you at six."

I get out of the car and wait for my mom to drive off, so I can have a smoke. But of course, she doesn't. She gestures towards the door.

I give her a thumbs up.

The door is unmarked, but there's a RingDNA doorbell. I press the buzzer and look into the camera.

"Hi. Can I help you?" a female voice answers.

"I'm here to, uhm, volunteer. I'm Debbie's daughter."

"Last name?"

"Rush."

"Common in. We need you to sign in at the office. Take a right once you get in the door."

The lock clicks. I open the door and follow the signs for the office.

"Alyssa?" The woman at the front desk slides me a clipboard.

"Yeah."

"We just need you to sign a few things. It's essentially saying that you understand that the women here are seeking temporary refuge, and you agree to protect their identities."

"Oh. Yeah of course."

"You did the training? Online?"

"Yeah. I did."

"You'll need to leave your belongings up here when you check in. No weapons, drugs or alcohol?"

"No. I mean, I have a pen," I blush a little.

"A pen?"

"Uh. A vape?"

"No worries," she locks my bag in a drawer under her desk, "I'm Christine."

"Nice to meet you."

"Maya's going to show you around today. She's one of our staff members." Christine reaches for the radio on her belt. "Maya, Alyssa Rush is here for you."

"Roger," says the voice on the other end.

I hear fast footsteps coming down the hall. I'm not ready to meet this kind of enthusiasm for the workplace.

"Well hello, Miss Rush," Maya clips the walkie talkie to her belt, "Follow me."

We speed skate down the winding hallways. I realize I'm in what was once an old Victorian home. It's ornate but not particularly well kept, one of those buildings that's entirely frozen in time. The walls are wallpapered, the carpets are paisley. Ragged posters adorn the walls–some inspirational, some educational. *Stroke. Know the Signs,* and *Kindness. Pass it On.* These too have seen better days.

"This the kitchen," Maya pauses at the island. She opens one of three industrial refrigerators. "Most of this comes from the food bank. One thing I got you doing today is checking expiration dates. Last thing we need up in here is salmonella. Old pipes." She winks.

"All the food is free. They can take what they want. You gonna be here Tuesdays?"

"Uh, maybe." I hope not.

"Tuesday's when we get the delivery," she shuts the fridge; the tour continues. "How many hours you got?"

I sigh, "A thousand."

"Damn girl. First offense?"

"Third."

Maya shakes her head. "Well if you ain't learned by now, you ain't ever gonna learn."

It's a thought I've had myself, actually. But I still resent her for saying it out loud. We walk up a back staircase, one that winds.

"What's this, like a secret passage?"

"Honey this is the *servant stairs*," she stops and lets that soak in.

I blush, "Oh I didn't…"

"Course you didn't. You white. White folk like to forget they built these back in *the day*."

At the top of the stairs is a long hallway. Each door is numbered with a small white board underneath. Some have names. *Diamond, Ashley, Rosario +2. Grace.*

"What does the plus two mean?" I ask.

"Means she brought two kids with her."

I nod.

"This room needs turning over," she points to door number three. "That's what you'll be doing first. Then the expiration dates."

Maya knocks on a door at the end of the hall. "Darren. Alyssa Rush reporting for duty," she announces.

The door opens, and I immediately wish I'd put on different clothes.

A dazzling smile, "Thank you Maya." Maya clips off.

"Darren," he extends a hand, "Glad to have you, Alyssa. Come on in."

You know you're in trouble when a handshake makes you want to drop your panties on the spot. *You woke up in a pile of laundry,* I remind myself, *This man wants nothing to do with you.*

Except he's one of those men that makes you feel like he does. He shuts the door to is office and gestures to a chair across from his desk. *Oh god.* We're about to do a real interview. I can feel myself sweating. This wasn't part of the deal. Show up. Check the dates on canned tuna. Pray that you don't see anyone that you know. Be out.

"So tell me," he takes a seat, "Why Agape?"

"Well my mom—" I pause. How do I tell this man that I'm here because I crashed my fucking car? That regardless of his obvious sex appeal, I would not be here if it wasn't for that. I'm just doing time, man. That's my why.

"My mom really admires the organization, and, you know, how it helps women in need," I offer.

"Debbie has been a pleasure to work with. But why do *you* want to be here?"

I can feel myself grinding my teeth.

"You know honestly, I just want to make things right," I look at my sneakers. It's the most honest answer I can give him.

"And you think volunteering here is going to do that?" he asks.

"Well the judge seems to think so," I wring out my hands. "I got a DUI."

Darren nods. He knows. Debbie probably told him. Or he saw the paperwork.

"Well Alyssa, I can't say this will make things right with whomever you hurt," he pauses, "But it will make things right with the law. Can I count on you to show up?"

"You can count on Debbie," I smile a little.

"Well that, I believe. Your mom's a good woman."

"She's alright," I nod.

"I believe you're a good person too," he stands up and motions towards the door. "Good people do bad things, Alyssa. Most just don't get caught. And the ones that do, well, they're crucified."

"Good people learn their lesson the first two times," I say, more to myself than to Darren.

Darren places hand on my shoulder. It's the first time I've been touched in—well, months. And suddenly, I feel like I'm going to cry.

"I'll let Maya know you're ready for room three."

"Is there a bathroom?" I can barely get the words out. He points to a door at the end of the hall. I bolt.

It's a good cry.

CHAPTER TWO

Soft Time

If I've learned anything from being an alcoholic, it's that the government does not care that you're an alcoholic–so long as you don't drive a car. If they did, rehab wouldn't be so expensive.

After my second offense, I thought long and hard about going to rehab. I even researched it.

What I realized is that rehab is for the Lindsey Lohans of the world–not for people like me. Rehab is for people with health insurance and savings accounts. It's for people who can afford to pause their life.

Rehab is not for people who make 7.40 an hour plus tips.

I realize it probably sounds like I'm making up excuses for myself. I'm not. In fact, I hate myself. Which makes not drinking a lot harder.

I hate myself every morning I wake up with a headache, every time I look in my bank account, every time I check my phone after a binge.

And let me tell you something, when you hate yourself, it's pretty hard to find a fuck to give for anyone else. Even, as it turns out, abused and battered women.

This is going to sound terrible. But when my mom suggested I do my hours at Agape Women's Shelter, I thought, *at least you'll be around people who have it worse off than you.*

Maybe it would put things into perspective. *Hey, you're a raging alcoholic piece-of-shit, but at least you have a home. At least you aren't dating an abusive psychopath.*

Not so. Not the case at all.

My second shift is on a Sunday. Debbie offers to swing by on her way home from church. This time, I'm ready. I'm even wearing eyeliner, the winged kind that shows you put a bit of effort in. Or whatever.

I check in with Christine like an old pro, handing her my bag. She radios for Maya. This time, instead of footsteps rounding the bend, Maya replies, "Send her to six."

"Do you remember the way?" Christine smiles.

I nod, but the answer is *barely.* The house is a maze. I decide I'll take my sweet time. I find the servant staircase easy enough. But this time, I decide to go down.

I love the smell of basement. It's so guttural, so earthy, so absolutely grounding. This basement is finished, so the scent is somewhat subdued by the drywall, the paint—whatever polyester the carpet was made from. This part of the house was finished last. It's industrial, not like the rest of the place. The ceiling is made of tiles, the kind you'd see in a midwestern office building.

I walk down a short corridor. Most of the doors are locked. I touch each doorknob gingerly, meeting resistance each time. The end of the hall opens into what must be a rec room.

For the first time, I notice that I'm not alone. A woman lays on a black leather couch. There's a baby on the floor beside her and an older child in the corner. The TV is on. A children's show is playing, but the volume is very soft. The woman scrolls through a social media feed.

"Hi," I offer.

She looks in my direction and nods in acknowledgement.

The older child cries out, "Mom. Mom look."

The woman on the couch turns towards him.

"Look. Watch," he insists.

She resumes scrolling.

"Mom," more urgently, "Look. Look! Like at McDonalds." He presses the buttons on a play cash register.

I feel myself becoming increasingly uncomfortable.

"Like at McDonalds?" I offer, gingerly approaching.

But he's not interested in me. I can go fuck myself. "Mom," he repeats, " Mom look."

She double-taps a meme.

"Mom!"

I slip away, back down the hall, like I was never there.

As I retrace my steps back towards the stairs, I hear a soft moan behind one of the locked doors.

I pause, listening intently.

Then the sound of heavy panting. I press my ear on the door. Another soft moan. The sounds of wet lips, breath, shuffling. Then suddenly, "Does anyone know where Alyssa is?"

Maya's voice, shrill and bothered, comes through a walkie talkie behind the locked door.

"Damn" I whisper under my breath.

I walk backwards towards the stairs as quickly and as quietly as I can manage.

Maya stands in room six with a hand on one hip. She's sweating.

"You get lost, or what?" she rolls her eyes, wiping sweat from her forehead. She's holding a sponge in her right hand and a bottle of cleaning spray in her left. The room is sparsely furnished—just a bed and a dresser. The wall facing the dresser has been vandalized, and I suddenly realize why Maya's perspiring.

"FUCK THIS HELLHOLE" the wall facing the dresser reads.

"Who did that?" I ask, my eyes widening.

"Alicia," Maya shakes her head, "Crazy bitch."

I wonder how politically correct it is to call a "battered woman" a crazy bitch.

"Why?" I take the cleaner from Maya.

"Oooh girl. Shit if I know. Took off this morning. Just like that," Maya snaps her fingers.

"Can't we just paint over it?" I ask.

"We gonna scrub off as much as we can first," Maya points to a roller in the corner, "And then *you* gonna paint over it."

I nod. "Cool."

"Come get me when you're through."

I start scrubbing at the paint. This shit is not coming off.

I work for about an hour before I decide to get Maya. She's in the break room next to the kitchen. She looks–haggard.

"I feel like I should just start painting over it," I say.

Maya jumps, "Jesus Christ. Walk a little louder next time." She clutches at her chest.

"You okay?" I ask.

"I'm good."

"You look–"

"Hmm?" Maya's eyebrows raise.

"Just tired. You look a little tired."

"Well honey. I am tired. Up all night."

"Shit. Doing what."

Maya hesitates.

"Sorry. It's none of my business," I back off.

"Nah. It's good." She looks around. "I was just up late earning some extra cash."

"Nothing wrong with that," I smile, "You have two jobs?"

Again, she looks around. "Take a break for a sec," she slides the chair next to hers towards me.

I'm more than happy to accept. My right shoulder is tight from scrubbing.

"I've been playing a game online," she confides, "On Saturday nights."

"Like poker?" I ask.

"Not really."

"Gambling?"

"Nah. It's a VR game. Virtual Reality."

"You make money doing that? You must be pretty good," I'm a little surprised, to be honest. Maya does not look like the gaming type. I guess mostly because she's not a four hundred pound man. But what do I know?

"Uh uh." she shakes her head, "I'm not that good."

I raise my eyebrows.

She laughs, "Well, I'm alright. But it's not what you thinking. We aren't live streaming on youtube or nothing."

"What game is it?"

Maya lowers her voice, "You ain't gonna tell?"

"Sure."

"It's just called *The Game*. I log in once a week and my character gets a mission."

"Who's your character?"

"It changes every so often, but right now I'm a sixteen year old kid."

"So you like… go to high school? Or what?"

"Yeah, but I always gotta do something."

"Like what?" I ask.

"Like yesterday, I had to steal a bag of chips out of the cafeteria."

I laugh, "Did you do it?"

"Hell yes I did!"

"And you get paid for this? For stealing fake chips from a fake school."

Maya can hear the skepticism in my voice. "Yeah," she continues, "But not all the missions be like that. Last week I had to kill a kid."

"What?"

"Week before, I had to cheat on a chem test."

I'm laughing now, "Okay and how much are they paying you?"

"$400 a night, give or take."

I nearly choke.

"You've got to be kidding me."

"Nope, this is the real deal. How you think I got these?" She points to her sneakers, fresh, uncreased, barely worn.

"Damn," I suck my teeth. I'm doing math in my head.

You can't live off of $400 a week–not really. But Maya said she's only doing this one night a week.

"Can you do more than one shift a week?" I ask.

"Uh uh." She shakes her head, "Just the one."

I look at the clock.

"You about ready to start painting?" Maya asks.

"Hold up." I can't *not* ask. "How'd you get this gig anyway?"

Maya smirks, "Why. You want in? Bet you got all kinds of fines to pay off."

She's not wrong. My stomach knots, in fact, at even the mention of the crippling debt I owe society.

In addition to the hours of community service, I'll spend the next five years paying off thousands in dollars in debt.

Fines. Legal fees. The degree I didn't finish. I try not to think about it too often. It's the type of shit that makes you feel utterly hopeless, like you might as well just give up. It's the type of shit that makes you want to–well, drink.

"You have no idea," I sigh.

"You want to play? There's a signing bonus." Maya winks.

"How much?" I ask.

"A grand."

This all sounds too good to be true. "What's the catch?"

"Let's paint and talk," Maya stands up abruptly, "I'm not trying to stay late to turn that room."

We make our way up to room six. My mind is spinning. Maya hands me a roller. She pours paint into a tray, almost carelessly–almost.

"If you want to play, there are a few rules. They ain't complicated, but you can't mess up."

"Got it," I start rolling.

"First off. You gotta be on time. No call-offs or you're done. Headset's on by the time your shift starts. Period."

I nod.

"Second," Maya continues, "If you quit, you have to pay back any bonuses you got that year. Same goes if you're kicked off. All of it."

"Put it on my tab," I shake my head.

"Seriously though. These folks ain't like the IRS. They're not sending you warning letters–they're coming for their money."

I nod. So maybe it *was* too good to be true.

"Last. The headset is–well it's state-of-the-art technology."

"Sweet."

"Kind of," Maya pauses. "Sometimes."

"What?"

"When you put that headset on, you can feel everything that happens in *The Game*," she pauses to let that soak in.

"So if someone slaps me–" I offer.

"It's gonna hurt."

"And when you killed that kid–"

Maya turns away, "I've only died once. But. It was not pleasant."

"How do you know this stuff isn't, like, causing irreversible damage?"

Maya laughs, "I guess I don't. But to be fair, I always feel fine the second the headset comes off. No side effects. On God." She places her hand on an invisible bible.

"No bruises? Cuts? Scars?"

"Nah. Not the kind you can see," she answers.

"Okay," I'm uneasy.

"Not all of it's bad, either. Before I was this kid, I was a sushi chef. You ever had sushi before?"

I nod.

"Well I hadn't," Maya said. "Tried it for the first time in *The Game*." She starts painting again. I follow suit. "The next day, I stop into a sushi spot. I need to know if it's the same."

"Was it?" I ask.

"Spot on." Maya replied. She shakes her head.

"That's–" I pause, "It's really kind of unbelievable."

"Who you tellin?" Maya scoffs. "So. You still in?"

I hesitate. "I don't know Maya. This all just sounds, well–"

"Hm?"

"A little suspicious. No offense."

"I get it." Maya nods. "It's not for everyone. Just thought you could use some extra cash, is all."

We paint in silence for about twenty minutes.

Finally, I cave. "How do they pay you?"

Maya smiles, "Direct deposit, baby. It's legal, too. Right after your shift. Like clockwork."

"Okay." I nod, resolutely.

She looks thrilled, "Okay?"

"I'll do it."

"Oh one last thing," Maya stops. "This thing needs to stay on the downlow. Can't nobody know you're playing. Got it? Not your family–not even your friends."

"I don't have any friends."

It's not a lie.

CHAPTER THREE

Duro Ventures

Maya collects my information. She tells me to check my email later for a message from Duro Ventures. They'll want to set up a consultation call to go over terms and conditions. Basically everything she already told me.

I finish painting and clean up as best I can. My clothes are covered in paint, and I regret wearing something nice to please a man I didn't even see. Debbie is waiting for me in the parking lot.

"Saw you went grocery shopping yesterday," she brings it up all too casually.

My mother and I have a joint bank account. She and my father loaned me the money I needed to pay the lawyer and my last month's rent. And the fee to break my lease.

Now she gets to see every dime that comes in and out of my life.

"Yeah. Just needed a few things to get by 'til I move."

"Did you save the receipt?" she asks?

"It's on the fridge." I answer.

This was one of the many strings attached to bailing me out. I need to account for my expenses. And of course, no alcohol.

The last bit was court-ordered, but Debbie-enforced. What she doesn't know is that I have about $72 of cash stashed in my room. And if that's not enough to get me messed up for a few days, well I'm doing something wrong.

We walk into the apartment, and she inspects the receipt.

Oreos - $3.72
Top Ramen - $.75
Pantene - $6.79
Kashi Granola - $5.49

She pauses when she gets to the granola. "You know you'd save a lot if you'd just buy the store brand. It's the same thing."

"It's my money, Mom," the words fly out of my mouth without thinking.

"It's our money, Lyss."

"So every paycheck I get now is your money?"

"Until you pay us back, yes."

I roll my eyes. She rolls her eyes.

"Do you want me to file this somewhere? Does Dad need to be involved in the audit?"

She shakes her head and walks out. "I'll see you on Wednesday." She slams the door.

Two days of sweet, sweet freedom.

I wait 'til the car is down the street and around the corner before I take off.

I can remember distinctly the first time I was drunk. It was amazing, euphoric. I was eighteen, which I guess is kind of old.

I'd had sips here and there before that. Nothing crazy. I was actually a pretty good kid.

I remember my high school health teacher telling us about binge drinking. I remember her saying that it was fine to consume alcohol in moderation, but you shouldn't be drinking to get drunk.

That night, that first night, as the world began to slow and my mind began to spin, I wondered if anyone out there is legitimately drinking for any other reason than to numb, to float, to disassociate.

I don't believe it.

The difference between me and everyone else is that most people have an off switch. And I don't.

The off switch is so far past the point of blacking-out that it may just as well not exist.

I'll drink until I can't sit up straight, 'til I physically can't keep going. This is why, for the most part, I like to drink alone. I don't, under any circumstances, want to be reminded of what I did the night before.

There is nothing more horrifying than watching a video of yourself from a party where you were gone before you even walked in the front door. It feels like it's someone else. But it's you. You ate an entire pizza. You threw up in your classmate's guest bed. You texted that guy from the yogurt spot. You took the $47 Uber to the liquor store.

You drove home.

You crashed your car.

"That wasn't Alyssa," my friends would say, "That was Francesca."

Francesca is my alter-ego. She's my scapegoat. It started out as a joke.

The worst part is that when it's time to pay the piper, Francesca's never around.

Honestly? Fuck Francesca. Fuck me.

******

I walk into the liquor store down the street from my place. The guy at the register is new.

I pretend to shop around for a little bit. This is an act. I know exactly what I want. But I feel like "people who don't drink to get drunk" probably shop around for a bit.

I pick up a six pack of Coronas. 4.5% ABV. Pass. Major pass.

I admire a top-shelf cabernet. This would absolutely fit the bill, but it's $28.98. Too rich for my blood.

"Anything I can help you find?" the cashier offers.

"I usually like a pinot noir," I scrutinize another bottle, "But I'm having people over. Maybe a box?"

"Over there," he gestures to the bargain section.

"Over there?" I pretend to look around. The charade continues.

I pick up the box version of pinot noir like I haven't bought this same, exact product six separate times this very month. God I'm a phony. But such is life. We're all acting most of the time, after all.

Box wine is my drink-alone poison of choice. Why? Three reasons.

1. It's cheap. And as you've probably already gathered, I'm incredibly broke. Now more so than ever. Ironically, in part, because of box wine.
2. You really can't tell how many drinks you've had. Have I had four small glasses or two large ones? One bottle or three? Who's to say? That number is between the box and whatever entity you call God.
3. It's actually not that bad. And although my doctor has made it very clear that this isn't the case, I like to believe the antioxidants counteract the liver damage.

I walk home with my little treasure swinging in a black plastic bag.

These nights have a comfortable, familiar rhythm to them.

Glass one. I do some light tidying. I even throw a load of laundry in the wash. I'll forget about this later. Hence the bare mattress.

Glass two. I scroll through my social media feeds. I like to get this done early on. Later is dangerous. For obvious reasons.

Glasses three to five. I usually turn the TV on. It'll stay on for the rest of the night, the soft glow of the screensaver illuminating the room.

Glass six. Soft porn.

Glass seven. Binge eat whatever I have on hand.

Glass eight. Pass out.

Only this night is different. This night involves a blip in the program, a glitch in the matrix. On this particular night, I check my email.

Now, to be honest, by the time I walked in the door, I'd all but forgotten my conversation with Maya. I couldn't tell you what possessed me to check my email. But I did. And sure enough, there, at the top of my inbox, was a message from Duro Ventures.

Subject: Hey Alyssa! Let's play.

Dear Alyssa,

You're receiving this missive on behalf of Maya Evans. We trust that as a fellow player, Maya has done an excellent job outlining the rules and parameters of The Game.

In order to take part in this exciting opportunity, we ask that you schedule an onboarding call within the next twenty-four hours. Click here *to schedule with Kyle, a fellow player and onboarding specialist.*

In preparation for your call, please review the attached contract and complete the W2. Your signing bonus will be direct-deposited within 2-3 hours of your onboarding.

Keep in mind that this is a one-time offer.

We look forward to playing with you!

Happy Winning,
Team Duro

I review the contract haphazardly. For the most part, everything seems to align with what Maya told me earlier. One shift a week. A grand for signing. Confidentiality. Blah blah blah.

It still seems way too good to be true. But they haven't asked me to put in my credit card number. What's the worst that could possibly happen?

I click the link to book an appointment with Kyle. His latest available booking is 11 a.m. Pretty early for me.

And the rest?

Well the rest is history.

CHAPTER FOUR

Onboarding

I hear the soft vibration of my phone against the baseboards. Slowly, clumsily, I slip my hand between the bed frame and the wall. I encounter what feels like a cheeto and recoil instantly.

Why am I such a slob?

Take two. I avoid the roach bait and successfully locate the phone, silencing it.

I attempt to pull it up to the bed, but my fisted hand is too big.

Jesus.

I roll off the bed and get on my hands and knees.

Gingerly, I reach in the direction of the phone.

Two missed calls. Neither one is from an area code I recognize.

Maybe my credit card bill is past due.

Suddenly, a light goes on. My onboarding call.

The adrenalin of missing what feels like an interview is enough to snap me back into this dimension. I grab my glasses from my dresser and hit redial.

Three rings.

"Ms. Rush?" a voice on the other end asks.

"Hi. Yes this is.. She. It's me."

"Please confirm your date of birth and the last four digits of your social."

"December 12, 1991. 5489."

"Thank you. Please hold."

The hold music is surprisingly upbeat. It's a pop song I couldn't tell you the name of but have heard a million times. I need water.

I stumble into the kitchen.

First. Advil.

I wonder if I have time to run to the gas station for a coffee.

"Miss Rush?" the operator is back.

"Yes."

"Kyle will take your call now."

"Thank you."

Silence, and then, "Alyssa Rush?"

"Yes."

"I'm Kyle. I'll be processing your onboarding. Please note that this call is being recorded. Do I have your permission to proceed?"

"Okay."

"I need a verbal yes or a no."

"Oh. Yes."

"Thank you," he pauses. Looks like all your paperwork is in. We appreciate that."

Thank you, Francesca. I owe you one. "No worries," I answer.

"I just need to review a few things with you on the line before we ship your equipment. Are you of sound mind?"

"I hope so," I laugh a little.

"If you agree, I'll need a verbal 'Yes.'"

"Oh. Uhm. Yes. I'm of sound mind."

"Good. We'll review the contract now."

"Alright," I'm uneasy. I'm sweating. But maybe it's just hanxiety.

"Part one deals with the equipment. Should you choose to sign your contract, you'll receive a headset and controller within twenty-four hours. This equipment is property of Duro Ventures and is tracked at all times. You must play The Game from the residence listed on your account. Do you understand?"

"Yes."

"Perfect. Part two deals with confidentiality. Your participation in The Game is confidential. When you first log in, you'll be assigned a character, an alter-ego if you will. Your relationship with this character must not be discussed with anyone outside of The Game. Your identity in The Game and your identity outside of The Game must be completely separate."

"What about Maya?" I ask.

"Maya?"

"The girl who recruited me. The *woman* who recruited me," I correct myself.

"Maya should not know your character," he pauses, "Nor should you know hers."

"Okay," I deliberate. I don't mention that I already know that Maya is playing as a sixteen year old chip bandit.

"While it's rare," Kyle continues, "You may encounter another Player outside of The Game. If your identity is revealed, you must Disclose. You'll do this prior to your shift."

"How?" I ask.

"I'm getting to that."

I've decided I don't like Kyle. Truly. He's an ass.

"Okay."

"Every time you clock in, you'll be given the opportunity to Disclose. If you select 'yes,' you'll be asked for the legal name and geographic location of the person you've encountered. Note that if another Player discloses and you do not, we'll be forced to conduct an investigation. If we find that you've wrongfully withheld Disclosure, you'll be terminated immediately. Do you understand?"

"Okay," I say.

"I need a—"

"Yes," I interrupt. "I get it."

"Perfect. Part three involves termination. If you're terminated, be it voluntary or involuntary, you'll be required to return your equipment and pay back any bonuses you've received. Please note that the headset is valued at twenty-five thousand US dollars. Note that you may choose to terminate at any time. You are an at will employee. Do you understand?"

"Yes."

"Thank you. Part four deals with compensation. When you log in for your shift, you'll be given a mission. Your shift is four hours in duration; however, you may be given multiple shifts to accomplish a mission. In either case, you'll be compensated at a base rate of $100 per shift plus a bonus for completing the mission."

I do the math in my head. "So it's actually $25 an hour?" I ask.

"If you don't complete the mission, yes. If you do complete the mission, you'll be compensated at a rate of $50 an hour or more—depending."

"Depending on what?"

"Depending on various bonuses and incentives," Kyle replies coldly. "Do you understand?"

I don't. I truly have no idea what he's talking about anymore. "Yes." I lie.

"Thank you," Kyle says. "Part five deals with withdrawals. At the end of the shift, you'll have the opportunity to withdraw from your earnings. It's advised that you withdraw no more than 50%, as the money you earn can be used to barter within The Game. Do you understand?"

"No. I really don't."

"At certain points in The Game, you'll have opportunities to make purchases that will increase the likelihood of accomplishing your mission. Do you understand?"

It's still a no but, "Yes."

"Thank you. Last, as Maya most certainly revealed to you, the headset is a state of the art piece of equipment, one designed to give you and all our Players an experience that mimics the world we live in to a degree never before imagined. You will see, hear, taste, smell and feel everything through your headset. Some of these experiences will be enjoyable. Others will be uncomfortable. While the pain you feel in The Game is temporary, we must be clear. The Game is not responsible for any emotional distress caused by participation, as participation is voluntary. Do you understand?"

I'm silent. I don't know if it's the hangover or the Advil or the coffee finally (finally) kicking in. But suddenly I'm sick to my stomach.

"Alyssa," Kyle repeats, "Do you understand?"

"Look." I take a deep breath, "I'm not really sure this is right for me. It all just sounds like–a lot."

The line is quiet.

"Hello?" I say.

"That's fine. I'll cancel the transaction."

"I'm sorry?" I say. "What transaction?"

"Your signing bonus. It's already been transferred to your account."

I tap my online banking app and sign in. There it is. $1000.00 even. *Pending*.

"Wait." I pause. What's the worst that could happen?

"I need a verbal yes or no."

"Yes."

And I sell my soul to the highest bidder.

CHAPTER FIVE

The Headset

I hang up the phone. I want to text Maya and let her know that I signed my contract. I kind of want her to talk me down, actually, tell me everything is going to be alright–the onboarders *have* to say that stuff.

But I can't open my text messages. Besides, I don't have Maya's number.

The truth is I haven't opened my text messages since the accident. I can't.

The first few days, when I was still in the hospital, I watched that little red number grow. Eventually, it plateaued. And now it hovers just over a hundred.

At least half, I can only assume, are Debbie. The rest are ghosts.

Ghosts are people from a past life. It's what my friend Molly used to call anyone who was "dead to her." This generally meant men who no longer served her, but it also included her biological father and a few girls who had dared to cross her in the eighth grade.

Once a ghost, it was as if you didn't exist in Molly's world. She had the willpower of a Tibetan monk. She didn't block people either. She didn't have to. She just canceled them.

We'd be studying at the kitchen island as her phone lit up again, and again, and again.

"Who's that?" I'd ask.

"Oh you know. Just a ghost."

"Which one?"

"Steven."

"Which one is Steven?"

"You know. Whole Foods Steven."

"No," I feign surprise. So Whole Foods Steven had gone the way of the world.

"Yes. I had to."

"No more free soaps." I shrug. This was a pity, for me at least.

"They weren't free Alyssa. He stole them."

"What'd he do?"

"He blew me off on Friday."

"In what sense?" It was important to clarify with Molly.

"On Thursday he asked what I was doing on Friday. I told him I didn't have anything going on. And he didn't text me back til Sunday afternoon."

This actually felt pretty valid. Molly's turned men to ghosts for far less. Last week, a dude she'd hooked up with nine times "asked if he could go raw." Ghost.

The week before, one of our mutual male friends told her she'd been "eating good." Ghost.

"Am *I* still allowed to talk to him?" I'd asked, referring to our mutual friend.

Her look said it all: don't associate with the ghosts unless you're prepared to be one.

"It just seems a little cruel, Mol," I tried coaxing her. "I actually think it was a compliment."

"How is it a compliment to call someone fat." A rhetorical question.

The first time she explained the concept to me, I furrowed my eyebrows. "Aren't *you* the ghost then? I mean you're ghosting him."

"I'm not going to be a ghost in my own life, Alyssa," she said matter-of-factly. To be fair, her way did make more sense.

Molly was my best friend. Now she's a ghost. And so am I.

Those 100+ text messages haunt me daily. But I'm not brave enough to face my ghosts. Or my demons. I'd rather hide under the covers and sleep.

There are some mornings where my body feels so heavy, I don't think I'll ever be able to leave my bed. It feels like I'm made of stone. I imagine an investigator peeling back the covers on my bed only to reveal a corpse lying on a bare mattress. How pathetic. How utterly embarrassing.

I've felt like this for a while, actually, the overwhelming burden of existence. And to answer your question, yes, I know that sounds dramatic. But it's genuinely how I feel. Heavy.

There is no true reason for this. I'm not a victim of trauma. I wasn't molested as a child. No one I care about has died suddenly or tragically. I have no ailments or maladies to speak of. Other than crippling depression.

Sure, my parents were religious, but that accounts for like three out of every ten nineties babies.

The truth is I have no idea what's wrong with me or why I am the way I am. I don't know why I'm an alcoholic.

Debbie thinks it's because I'm directionless, but that's not true. Or it wasn't true. In fact, Molly and I were studying for our LSATs before I crashed.

It's more true now, but it's a symptom—not the cause.

In any case, not having to friggin' scrounge for every cent I have to my name certainly wouldn't hurt.

You know what blows? Being thirty and poor. When I was in my early twenties, I used to tell people I didn't care about money. And I believed that. I believed that chasing money was inherently vile and so base.

Boy was I ever brainwashed.

Before I lost my license, I used to drive through nice neighborhoods and just people-watch. Half the women looked my age—if not younger. And they're out here pushing double-wide baby carriages and walking their labradoodles in leggings that cost more than two week's worth of groceries.

What are they doing that I'm not? Where did I go wrong?

I got my bachelors in literature. I guess that was mistake number one. No one is going to pay you to read books. They should put *that* on a plaque above the department office.

After I graduated, I became—well a waitress, of course. And eventually a bartender. And a nanny and dog walker and call center employee and house cleaner and whatever else I could cobble together to pay rent in my dumpy little one-bedroom apartment.

After my second DUI, I decided I probably couldn't keep working in "the industry." And for what it's worth, it helped. For a bit.

I was sleeping normal hours and generally avoiding dens of thieves Monday through Thursday. On Fridays and Saturdays, we'd dress up and go out and yes, black out. But it was pretty manageable and weirdly acceptable to do in those days. Everyone did it.

But eventually, most of my friends found "their person" (I hate that phrase). Some got married. Some had kids. Most shacked up and stayed in. And then it was just me and Molly.

We both had serious and not-so-serious relationships in our twenties. I dated one guy for three years, actually.

Breaking up with him? That was mistake number two.

The irony is that I broke up with him because he was too ambitious. And I was really scared of that. Everytime he did something healthy and good for himself, I just felt worse and worse about myself. He'd get up after a crazy night out and go straight to the boxing gym.

I never said it out loud, but I really resented him. For doing and being all the things I couldn't. For having this drive and passion and purpose. I really hated him for that.

Oh and he cheated on me. But that's besides the point. When I found out, I was actually relieved.

I was going through his phone to check his bank account, actually. More out of curiosity than anything else. And as I'm trying to guess his online banking password (what was his mom's dog's name?), he gets this text.

"Tonight?" with a little heart. A black heart. A sexy-girl, I-know-the-answer-is-yes heart.

The number isn't saved.

I didn't even open the text. If it smells fishy, it is. That's what my grandad used to say.

"What are you doing?" he asked, a towel wrapped around his narrow waist.

I tossed the phone on his bed.

"What did you say you were doing tonight?" I asked.

"I have plans with David" he looked worried now.

I rolled my eyes. "Well I hope you last longer with David." It was the meanest thing I could think of. And also the last thing I ever said to him.

Lie to me? Ghost.

When I told Molly, she was half upset. She was single, so this news was advantageous to her.

"Let's get shitfaced. Hook up with someone. Make him really regret it."

As if we needed an excuse.

***

My headset arrives within twenty four hours of signing my contract. I guess it must have arrived overnight, which doesn't strike me as odd for whatever reason. I suppose it should have. But it doesn't.

The box is clearly marked "HANDLE WITH CARE. EXTREMELY FRAGILE."

What *is* odd is that I didn't have to sign for the package. My neighborhood is notoriously ridden with porch pirates, which is why I almost always had my stuff shipped to Molly's.

I'm relieved to find the package untampered with, and I tentatively bring it into the kitchen. I push a pizza box to the side and carefully begin to slide my keys through the packing tape.

Inside the brown shipping box is a matte black package. It's pristine, immaculate. I wonder if I have to save this. Probably.

I slide it out carefully and remove the cover.

The headset is as big as a motorcycle helmet and also a matte black. It's huge. I guess I was anticipating a pair of goggles. I've never seen anything like it before. Maybe on TV, but not in real life.

The back of the helmet extends further than the base of the skull, terminating at a point that looks like it will land just at the base of the neck.

I pick it up. It's remarkably light.

I dig through the circus peanuts until I find a pamphlet. OPERATING INSTRUCTIONS.

It's about 100 pages long.

"Christ," I mutter under my breath, only to realize that the instructions have been translated into fifty languages or more. The English section is only three pages in length.

I begin to read.

Operating Instructions

Please note, headset and controller are fully charged upon delivery.

Important: Headset will lock in place once on the head. The sensation can cause claustrophobia in some users. Rest assured that the headset will unlock after your shift.

We recommend having a light meal, including water, prior to your shift. During your shift, you will find it difficult to use the restroom and impossible to eat or drink. Plan accordingly.

In between shifts, the headset can be charged by placing it on the charging dock (included). Please place the charging dock in a private and secure location.

The Game must be played in a private and secure location. If a private and secure location is not available, you are not eligible for participation.

The headset is equipped with unlimited high speed data. No internet connection is required to play. The headset pairs via bluetooth with the controller (included).

While the headset is relatively low maintenance, occasionally bodily fluids will need to be removed from the headset interior and/or controller. For this reason, we've included a cleaning kit designed to safely cleanse and sanitize the devices. Please do not use any other solvents, as they may damage the equipment.

To confirm receipt, please put the headset on within twelve hours. Your first session will last no longer than sixty minutes and is designed to confirm your identity and orient you to The Game. Again, plan your bodily needs accordingly.

Welcome to The Game!

When I get to the part about the headset locking, I feel my stomach turn.

"It'll be fine," I try to console myself.

I look at my watch. It's noon. By my estimation, I have about four hours til the 12 hour deadline is up.

I walk to the counter to feel the weight of the box wine. It's light but not empty. I pour myself a glass to take the edge off. I drink it like a glass of water–quickly. And immediately I feel better.

Even though the alcohol hasn't hit my brain, my blood, I feel better. Just knowing it will hit me makes me feel safer and more equipped to handle the unknown.

"Here goes nothing," I put the headset on.

Immediately the screen lights up.

PLEASE SIT DOWN. The words flash on the screen several times. I feel around for the back of a chair.

I sit.

The message disappears.

A robotic female voice, "Hello. Welcome to The Game. During this session, we'll orient you to your new headset. Please state your name starting with your first name."

"Alyssa Rush." I stutter.

"Thank you. Please verify your date of birth and the last four digits of your social security number. If you don't have a social security number, say, 'I don't have one.'"

I provide the credentials.

"Thank you for verifying your identity. My name is Lia. You can speak to me in complete sentences. From this point forward, we'll use facial recognition technology to verify your identity. Under no circumstances should any other person wear your headset. Do you understand? Please say yes or no."

"Yes."

"Thank you. Have you read the Operating Instructions?"

"Yes," I say.

"Thank you. Let's get started. Are you ready to begin your shift?"

"Yes."

"Thank you. Your headset will now lock."

The screen lights up. HEADSET LOCKING IN 5... 4... 3...

I hold my breath.

2... 1... Click.

"I have sensed that your heart rate has risen above 120 beats per minute. It's normal to feel anxious during your first shift. Take a deep breath," the OS instructs.

I begin to breathe in.

"Breath out to the count of six. Six, five, four, three, two, one."

ANALYZING flashes on the screen.

"These are your bioanalytics," Lisa continues.

Heart rate: 115 bpm
Blood Alcohol: .07
Blood Pressure: 100/80
Blood oxygen: 97

"I have sensed that your blood alcohol is just under the legal limit. Please note that if your blood alcohol is over the legal limit, you will not be eligible to play. Do you understand?"

"Yes." Bummer.

"Thank you. This session is divided up into two parts. During the first thirty minutes, you'll take a test to measure your IQ, EQ and spatial intelligence. Please place both hands on the controller. You may use either the controller or your voice to answer the questions."

I feel around on the table blindly for my controller. There it is.

"Let's begin. Please read the question on the screen. When you're ready to answer, please say your answer choice. The first question is a practice question."

The screen illuminates with a simple math problem.

$17+3 =$

    a. **10**
    b. **14**
    c. **21**
    d. **20**

"D." I say.

"Thank you. That's correct. The test will begin now."

I can feel myself sweating. I try to imagine if Maya had told me all this from the jump. I can tell you right now that I would not have been in. Hard pass. No. Too late now.

ASSESSMENT COMPLETE

"Would you like to know your score?" Lia asks.

"Not really," I roll my eyes.

"Thank you. Next, we'll begin to introduce you to your headset. As you know, this is a state of the art piece of equipment designed to seamlessly mimic the world you are playing in. Let's start with a familiar experience. Have you tried any of these fruits?"

An apple, raspberry and lemon appear on the screen.

"Yes. All of them."

"We'll start with the apple then. Use the controller to select the apple."

On screen, the apple appears to be bitten into. I hear a satisfying, crisp crunch. And then, like magic, I can taste it.

Moreover, I can *feel* it. The pressure of the fruit against my front teeth, the snap of the skin, the grain of the flesh on my tongue, the wetness of the juice as it fills my mouth.

"Holy mother fucking shit." I say right out loud.

"Now select the raspberry." Lia says.

This time the raspberry simply disappears. And as soon as it does, it's as if it's in my mouth. Each paper soft aril bursts under my molars. It's a perfect raspberry. The archetype. The platonic raspberry. And I realize, I've actually never had a raspberry this good. And I probably never will.

This raspberry, this fake raspberry, has ruined all other raspberries for me.

"Can I have another one?" I ask. "How does this even work?"

"Thank you for asking. You may not have another raspberry, however you may encounter them in The Game. The headset works through electrical impulses that stimulate the areas of your brain that light up during certain experiences. Select the lemon."

A wedge is cut from the lemon. Slowly the center softens, as if being bitten and sucked.

My mouth puckers as the acid coats my tongue. It's shockingly and terrifically unpleasant. I shiver and twitch.

"As you can see," Lia continues, "While some experiences in the game are pleasant, others are less so. The headset is also able to simulate pain. For example, let's see how it feels to stub your toe. This experience is ranked by players as a three out of ten on the pain scale."

A disembodied foot, bare, appears on the screen next to a wall. Without warning, the big toe crumples against the wall.

And I feel it. I feel it in waves. The first wave hits soft and the second is worse.

"Fuck! Goddamn!" I say out loud, wincing. "How high do the levels go?"

"Level ten pain experiences are rare but they do occasionally occur."

"But none of this is actually going to, you know, kill me... right?" I ask.

"No. Your headset continually monitors your vital signs, as you saw displayed at the beginning of your shift. Should your vital signs ever become alarmingly outside the realm of homeostasis, the headset will unlock. If the headset is not removed immediately, an ambulance will be called automatically."

"Okay, how often does that happen?"

"This has never happened. While players occasionally lose consciousness, their vital signs remain consistent. This is because in the same way that you didn't actually eat a raspberry, you didn't actually stub your toe."

"Okay," I say.

"Recall that many experiences will also be pleasurable. For example…"

A woman appears on the screen. She's older, a bit bigger. Right away, I can smell her. It's a mix of Red Door and Aquanet. She opens her arms wide and wraps them around me, tightly.

And all of the sudden, I'm crying. Maybe this is what they meant by bodily fluids. Tears, fat tears, are streaming down my face. Are they real?

"This concludes our first shift. Recall that you're an at will employee. Would you like to schedule consecutive weekly shifts? Please say yes or no."

"Yes."

"Please select a weekday for your shift."
"Tomorrow," I say quickly. "Wednesday."

"Absolutely. Thank you. We'll see you at 7 p.m. Eastern on Wednesday nights."

"Will that woman be there? In the game?"

"I don't understand the question."

"The woman who just…" I'm suddenly embarrassed. "Nevermind."

"Your headset will now unlock."

Click. I take the headset off and set it on the kitchen table. Tomorrow cannot come fast enough.

On Wednesday, Debbie picks me up for my shift. This time I'm waiting on the stoop.

"You look well-rested," she says.

This is the power of under-eye concealer and eight hours of sober sleep. The combination will take years off your age.

"I'm wearing make-up," I say, which immediately sounds dismissive. And I suppose it is. I hate being appraised, especially by my mother.

Something about being a woman makes it okay for everyone and anyone to comment on your appearance. It's bonkers. What's even crazier is that we're supposed to think these are "compliments."

I'm not a particularly pretty girl. I have no chest to speak of. My hair is a mousy brown and so are my eyes. I'd give myself a solid six out of ten.

Occasionally, I'll whip out my arsenal of drugstore dupes and "put a little effort in." Debbie's words, not mine. And whenever I do, the comments I get make me want to put a bag over my head.

"Well it looks nice," Debbie says. "Nothing wrong with putting a little effort in."

My mother hasn't left the house without a full face in years. Even in photos of my birth, her rouge is airbrushed high on her cheekbones. Debbie puts the effort in. In 1998, a friend introduced my mother to the Bare Minerals collection, and she has never gone back. She swears by that shit. To this day, she plucks her eyebrows into two slim, high arches. Mascara is a must, along with eyeliner–but never past the outer corner. And for special occasions, the smoky eye of course.

I find it so interesting how people get frozen in time. They find something that works and it's 'til death do us part.

I'd never tell her to her face, but she's actually quite lovely underneath the mask. Besides, I'm distracted.

I'm anxious to see Maya. I have a billion questions.

I jump out of the car, ring the bell and tap my foot against the concrete.

"Alyssa Rush," I announce before anyone even asks.

Christine buzzes me in and I dart down the hallway, handing her my forms.

"Oh we don't sign these til the end of the month," Christine redirects me.

"Is Maya working today?" I ask.

"Yeah. She left you a list."

"I was actually hoping to ask her a few questions," I interject.

Christine looks mildly concerned. "Is everything okay?"

"Oh definitely! I just–" think, Alyssa, "She was telling me about a job I might apply for."

When lying, I like to tell a partial truth. It's easier to weasel out of when the time comes. Whoever you lied to has to sort through which parts of the story are real and which are false, which is very disorienting.

Job. True.

Might apply for. Lie.

"I think she's in the rec room," Christine tells me. She hands me Maya's list, which I shove directly into my back pocket.

"Thanks," I take off.

But when I get to the rec room, Maya isn't there. She's not in the break room or the kitchen or the bathroom either. I've essentially searched the entire house without getting too close to the main office. Or to Darren's office.

See, I prefer not to lie. And if I encounter either Christine or Darren–I'll be forced to.

I decide to check the break room one last time, but this time, the door is locked.

I jiggle the handle. Definitely locked.

The door swings open abruptly. I jump. Maya looks perturbed.

"I'm sorry." I say.

"No worries," Maya says, "We just wrapping up."

Grace, swallowed by her giant cable knit sweater, squeezes behind Maya and walks quietly down the hall. She disappears into room two.

I step inside. Maya closes the door. She locks it. Her mood changes immediately. A mischievous smile spreads across her face. She's giddy.

"When's your first shift," she rubs her hands together.

"How'd you know?" I asked.

"Just a feeling. Don't know why else you'd be trying so hard to get in here–"

"Oh I'm sorry, I–"

"I'm just playing. So when is it?"

"Tonight."

"Ohhh baby girl get ready for that bread," she grabs a can of Pepsi from the fridge. "Do you mind?" she hands it to me. "I just got these done." Maya flashes a fresh full set of acrylic nails, square tipped and bedazzled.

I snap open the Pepsi and hand it to her. Those nails look, well, expensive. But I wouldn't know I guess. Mine are little nubs. She takes a sip.

"I was actually hoping I could ask you a few questions," I mention, trying to keep it casual.

"You ain't even started! What questions do you have?"

I can tell I'm going to get to ask one, *maybe* two..

"How do I get the bonuses?" I ask.

Maya motions to lower my voice. "Look. Like I said, all this is on the downlow. Didn't they tell you all this in orientation?"

"Well they said we get a base pay of $100 an hour. But I thought you said–"

"And more if you fulfill the mission."

"What's the mission." Question two.

"Like I said. It changes." She glances at the door. "Where's that list I gave Christine? Don't you have work to do?"

"Oh," I pull it from my pocket.

"Oven's not cleaning itself," she says.

I nod. Point taken.

The first item on the list is sheets for room two.

I have no idea where the clean sheets are, but I'm out of questions. Besides, I'm in no rush. What are they going to do? Fire me? I doubt it.

I begin my search on the second floor. I'm looking for a linen closet. Or a laundry room. Most of the unmarked doors are locked.

"Looking for something?" Christine asks. I nearly jump out of my skin.

"Sheets," I hold up the list, "For room two."

"Oh we keep those locked up. Some of the girls have sticky fingers."

I follow her to one of the doors I'd tried earlier. She uses her lanyard to unlock it.

"What's all that?" I ask, pointing to rows upon rows of toiletries.

"Oh those? Those are donations. We get a lot of donations." She opens a drawer. "These are hotel minis."

Some of it is really nice, too. Liters of Matrix, Aveda, Olaplex. I remind myself that it's not appropriate to feel jealousy towards victims of domestic violence. It's like wishing you could park in the handicapped spot.

Beneath the shampoos are two shelves of sheets, neatly folded and stacked.

"Take your pick," Christine says.

I grab a set of pink sheets, mainly because they're on top, but also because they look cheery.

"Thanks," I head down the hall.

When I get to room two, I knock on the door.

"Yes?"

"Uhm. I have your sheets," I say.

The door opens a crack, then all the way.

"Hi," the woman steps to the side. She winces. "I'm Grace."

She's small, but not short. Red hair frames her high, gaunt cheekbones. She's wearing a giant sweater, long enough to be a dress but too wide to be fashionable. She's wearing sweatpants and wool socks.

I can tell by her posture that she's favoring her right leg.

"Do you want me to put these on for you?"

She looks relieved, "If you don't mind. Yes."

She hobbles out of the way. I follow her in.

By the looks of it, she hasn't brought much with her. Two paper grocery bags by the door are filled with clothes and shoes.

"I had to leave pretty fast," she says, "A suitcase would have looked suspicious."

"You can sit," I say.

Grace sits down gingerly in the chair next to the dresser. Even that looks painful. She rolls up her sleeves, revealing two bracelets. They're Pandora bracelets.

"Those are pretty," I smile. They're not, but I don't know what to say.

"Thanks," she fingers them, "They're for my kids."

I smile and do my best to hook the corner of the fitted sheet over the mattress without cursing.

"I would have brought them," she pulls the sleeve back over the bracelets. "If I thought he'd hurt them, I would have brought them. I'm not like, a bad mom or anything."

"I wasn't thinking that," I reach for a pillowcase.

"They'll be at their grandma's eventually anyway. After I heal up. Do you have kids?"

"No," I say. I don't elaborate.

"That's good," she says. "Easier. I would have left years ago."

"I don't even have a boyfriend."

"That's good. I mean, do you have a girlfriend?"

"No. Just me."

"You know, my whole life I really believed that getting married was the best possible thing you could hope for. They really make it seem that way. How old are you anyway?"

"I'm thirty," I finish the bedding and stand back to admire my work. I can't remember the last time I made my own bed.

"You look young," she says. It sounds envious. I almost want to laugh. But then I'd have to confess that I'm only here because my life is a mess too. And I did it to myself.

On my way out of the building, Maya winks at me.

I smile. It's always nice to have someone looking out for you.

CHAPTER SIX

The First Challenge

Debbie rolls into a spot in front of my apartment.

"So," she pauses. I can tell she's been sitting on whatever she's about to say, and I immediately clench right up.

So…" I say.

"I saw you got a new job."

"Yeah." I confirm.

"Well that is just great. Where is it?"

"It's," think, Alyssa, think. "It's a remote thing."

"Oh?"

"Yeah. Actually I have a shift tonight."

I dash out the door. I know what she's thinking. Does this mean I can stay in my apartment? On $400 dollars a month? Hell. Fucking. No.

But if it's $400 a week, maybe. I've certainly eeked by on almost nothing in the past. And Maya did mention other bonuses.

I have a half hour before I'm locked in. I take a small (small) drink of gatorade and wonder if anyone's ever pissed themselves playing. I'm sure it's happened.

Finally, it's 6:55. Close enough. I grab the headset from the charging dock, sit down at my desk and put it on.

The screen turns on.

Welcome, Alyssa.

"Alyssa, are you ready to start your shift?"

"Yes"

"Headset will lock in five, four, three, two—" Click.

I take a sharp breath in.

"We'll now analyze your biometrics."

Heart rate: 100 bpm
Blood Alcohol: .00
Blood Pressure 100/80
Blood oxygen: 97

"These all fall in the acceptable range. Thank you. It's time to choose your character."

I feel my heart start to race.

"Keep in mind that these attributes are chosen at random. For each attribute, you'll be given one spin on the wheel."

A gameshow style spinner appears in the headset, floating in the virtual abyss.

"Based on your IQ/EQ test, you've been allotted 4 respins. Use them wisely. If you choose not to respin, you'll receive a $100 bonus per respin remaining. First spin for your gender. Say 'spin' when you're ready."

The spinner populates with pink and blue pie slices representing male and female. Not particularly progressive, but what can you do?

"Spin." I say.

The wheel is set in motion. Pink. Blue. Pink. Blue. Pink... Blue....... Pink.

"Female. Would you like to respin?"

I consider. It feels like a silly question. "Would you rather have more power, money, and respect?" But even if I respin, I might just get female again. And I have no idea what the other attributes are.

"No."

"Thank you. Next we'll spin for age. Say spin."

The wheel is transformed, each segment now featuring a number, ranging from twelve to ninety-nine. Some slices are bigger than others. Ninety-nine, for instance, is very small.

"Lia can I ask a question?"

"Yes."

"Why are some of the segments bigger?"

"The segments match the demographic breakdown in the United States in 2010. Does this answer your question?"

"Yes."

"Say spin." No small talk.

"Spin."

Again, my pulse quickens. I don't want to be some pre-pubescent twerp. No thank you.

35... 46...... 17......... 23.

"Twenty-three. Would you like to respin?"

Absolutely not. No. I try to imagine my life at twenty-three. I would sell my soul to be twenty-three again.

"No thank you."

"Perfect."

A twenty-three year old woman appears next to the spinner, a mannequin–hairless with grey skin.

"Now we'll spin for skin tone."

The wheel transforms, flesh-toned pie slices, again of various sizes.

"Spin."

The pointer lands on a dark, rich, brown.

"Would you like to respin?"

It's a loaded question. Would I like to be black in America?

The thought occurs to me. "Am I playing in America?" I ask.

"Yes. In this iteration of The Game, you'll be playing in New York, New York, USA."

"Respin." The respin counter in the bottom right of the screen moves from four to three.

Now I'm white. Or, rather, I'm not black. I suppose I could be Greek or possibly arab. But I'm not black. I breathe a guilty sigh of relief.

I spin for my height. 5' 6."

My weight. 134 lbs.

My hair. Chestnut brown.

My features. This one is strange. Each segment of the wheel features the face of a celebrity or well known person.

"Spin."

Angelina Jolie… Hillary Clinton…… Elizabeth Moss……… Megan Fox.

I gasp audibly. I can't fucking believe I get to live life as Megan Fox. Sure I'm a five foot six Megan. But I'm still Megan Fox.

Megan's impeccable face is miraculously transferred to my avatar's body, flawless makeup and all. Her perfect winged eyeliner. Her pouty soft lips. Her pencil straight nose. Her giant white teeth. She smiles. I smile. We smile.

"Re–"

"No." I cut Lia off.

I'm perfect. I'm gorgeous.

"Now you may choose a name to play under. Players need only to choose a first name. You may choose any name, however it may not be a variation of 'Alyssa' or 'Rush.'"

I think for a moment. I want a name that oozes femininity. A girl I went to high school with pops into my head. She was my lab partner–not by choice, of course. I remember distinctly that she was one of the first girls in school to have her own cell phone. Our biology teacher, Ms. Lee, took it one day when she was texting during the slide deck.

"That fat bitch," my lab partner rolled her eyes, "She's probably jealous. No one's texting her."

Ms. Lee was the smartest woman I'd ever met. And she was kind too. She was the kind of teacher who always handed the test back face down.

But if, in that moment, you'd asked me if I'd rather trade places with my lab partner or Ms. Lee, I'd have picked–

"Adrianna." I say out loud.

"Thank you, Adrianna," Lia says, "Let's review your mission." A timer appears in the bottom left of the screen. 3:44 and counting down. In the top left, I can see my pay, which currently sits at $400.

"Lia, can I ask another question?"

"Yes."

"Why do I have $400 in my account?"

"That's your base pay of $100 plus three remaining respins at $100, totaling $400."

"Right."

"View your mission at any time throughout your shift by saying 'Mission' or 'View Mission.'"

"Mission." I hold my breath.

An email of sorts opens in the center of my field of vision. It's dated and timestamped. The subject is "Mission One."

For this mission, your objective is to find a date for dinner. The date can be male or female but the dinner should be romantic in nature, ending with a kiss on the face or mouth. This mission is worth $300.

Receive a bonus of $200 if you secure a romantic date with a married individual. Receive a $400 bonus if the individual chooses to ask you out on a second date.

Maybe I won't have to move out after all. A date? This is a joke. I thought I was going to have to kill the president.

"Would you like to ask any clarifying questions about the mission?"

"Am I allowed to tell the person that I'm on a mission?"

"No. You may not disclose your mission to another player. Doing so will result in immediate disqualification and all daily bonuses will be revoked."

"Even the $300?"

"Yes. Upon disqualification, you'll receive your base pay of $100 for the completion of your shift."

"Will the headset unlock?"

"No."

Damn. "Do I get to at least, like, watch TV or something?"

"No."

So don't be disqualified. Noted.

"Would you like to ask any other clarifying questions about the mission?"

"No."

"Let's begin. Remember, if you'd like to view the mission, just say view—"

"Okay." The clock is ticking and I'm sweating.

The room begins to materialize. I'm in a bedroom, my bedroom, I guess. It's the bedroom you'd get if you asked a seven year old to draw a bedroom. The bed has four bedposts that end in traditional, carved wooden knobs. I actually can't remember if I've ever seen a bed like this in real life. Maybe in a cottage. Or in a photo of a cottage.

The walls are wallpapered. The bedside table has a single drawer and a lamp, which is on. There's a dresser facing the bed and a mirror hanging on the wall.

This looks like the bedroom in Blue's Clues, that TV show from the 90s.

It's simultaneously every room I've ever been in and no room I've ever seen.

On the nightstand next to the bed, a phone lights up. I walk to the closet, which is empty. A notification appears on screen.

PURCHASE CLOTHES?

"No," I say.

I wonder what I'm wearing now. I look in the mirror. Absolutely nothing. And I am fucking hot. Perfectly proportionate. Lifted. Smooth and tight. I am every woman and I am no woman. I am Megan Fox's face, Scarlet Johanson's chest, Kira Knightly's waist, Cardi B's ass, Naiomi Campbell's legs.

This is what I've wanted my whole life. This is awsome.

A hint appears on the screen.

HINT: CHECK YOUR PHONE FOR NOTIFICATIONS AND MESSAGES.

I turn to the phone on my nightstand, which lights up a second time. I pick it up. The screen fills my visual field.

An app in the bottom right of the screen blinks, drawing my attention to it. It's called Ember. Clever, I think to myself.

I tap the application to open it, and I'm immediately presented with the settings page.

The mission was to get a date. With anyone. So I set my gender preferences to "Anyone."

I drag the age parameters to a maximum of 55. Why not? It's not like I actually have to like these guys. Or… girls.

There are a variety of other filters that I leave set at their defaults. The clock is literally ticking.

Then I'm asked to choose my photos. Now here's the rub.

Choose something too sexy? You may as well be a hooker. Too genuine? You're in the friend zone. That whole "lady in the streets but a freak in the bed" thing has always driven me a bit bonkers. But hey, we live in a man's world. And based solely on the size of my breasts, I'd say this is a man's world too.

I open the camera on my phone. There it is, my perfect, hairless mannequin body. Guess these will have to be headshots.

Click. Click. Click. Three perfect selfies. We're off to the races.

A face appears on the screen, a digital baseball card.

SAY "RIGHT" TO SWIPE RIGHT OR "LEFT" TO PASS.

Eric, 29. Hobbies include fishing, hunting, and church. He looks like the kind of guy who would tell his buddies what color your pubic hair is the next day.

Just as I'm about to swipe left, I remind myself that this is a game. Funny how quickly I forgot.

"Right."

It's a match. Should I message him? No. Guys like this like to be the ones to make the first move. Guys like this want to penetrate your inbox. They want you to wait like a rabbit in a hutch 'til it's your turn to be played with.

But then the thought occurs to me: what if Eric, 29 is actually just another thirty-year-old white girl? I guess I'll never know.

Jamaal, 44 is looking for someone to settle down with.

"Right."

Martin, 27 is self employed, which in the real world means he's either a ride-share driver or going to try to get me to invest in bitcoin.

"Right."

Chris, 51, is married and just looking for something fun.

"Right."

I wonder if these are real people like me. Or if they're padding the deck with stock characters. Or bots. Or both.

Diane, 21 is in an open relationship.

"Right."

Wyatt, 34 owns a ferret.

Kill me, "Right."

Ahmed, 27 is just a regular guy who enjoys the simple things.

I roll my eyes. "Right."

It's a match. And a message.

AHMED: Hi gorgeous.

I check the time. I have just over two hours to seal the deal.

ADRIANNA: Hi handsome.

I *hate* myself for saying this. Alyssa would *never* say this. But Adrianna would. Or at least I think she would. I have no idea.

ADRIANNA: What are you up to?

AHMED: Not a whole lot. U?

How do I answer this? I have no idea what day of the week it is. I have no job.

Tell him you're sitting in the amalgamation of every room that ever was in a body that you would have traded your left kidney for.

No, Ahmed likes the simple things.

ADRIANNA: I'm just sitting here naked.

AHMED: Can't figure out what to wear, huh?

ADRIANNA: Actually I just don't have any clothes.

AHMED: LOL you must be new here?

ADRIANNA: Yeah. First day.

I immediately wonder if I'm allowed to tell people that.

AHMED: You have to buy something. Before you can leave the house.

ADRIANNA: Well I really have no reason to leave the house.

AHMED: I can fix that. Dinner? My treat.

That was easy. It's nice being Adrianna.

ADRIANNA: Sounds amazing. Where? And… how?

AHMED: Well first, buy yourself some clothes. Then you should be able to walk out the front door. Olive Garden or Red Lobster?

We're in New York city and we're eating at Red Lobster? What a waste.

ADRIANNA: Oh I love seafood. See you soon?

AHMED: I'm heading out now. I'm into heels by the way. ;)

I bet you are. Heels are modern foot binding. I keep that bit to myself.

I close the app and walk to my empty closet.

WOULD YOU LIKE TO PURCHASE CLOTHES?

"Yes." I say.

A list of stores populates on the screen as a series of icons.

Express. American Eagle. Urban Outfitters. H&M. J Crew.

Nice ones too. Balenciaga. Gucci. Saks.

"Hey Adrianna, if you'd like to search, just say 'search' and I'll help you out. You can also select a store by reading its name." Lia chimes in.

"How do I pay?" I ask.

"You have $400 in your account. Every US dollar counts for ten in the game. You have $4000 dollars."

I've never had four grand to my name in my life. I'm rich. I'm also bare-ass naked.

So buy a dress and heels, I think to myself. Easy.

"H&M." I say.

I pick out a little black dress, tight and tiny, and black ankle boots.

"Would you like to try on what's in your bag?" Lia asks.

Try it on? Nothing has sizes. I have a made to order body.

"Uhm. Do I have to?"

"No. All clothes purchased in The Game are sized to fit your avatar. Would you like to purchase the items in your bag?"

I look at the total. $78.34 USD. Eight real dollars for two immaterial items. That's half a box of wine, I work through the conversion.

"Yes."

"Thank you for your purchase! The items have been added to your cart. Would you like to keep shopping?"

Yes. Forever. Everything fits and it's 90% off.

"No." I say, reluctantly. Red Lobster awaits.

The dress and shoes sit in my closet, no tags.

I select them and put them on and walk towards my bedroom door.

I wonder what the rest of my house looks like. I walk to the door and open it.

There's my answer. This isn't a house at all. It's one of hundreds of rooms, each with identical doors. I guess I should probably check the number on my door.

853.

"Lia," I ask, "Do I need to lock the door?"

"You may lock any residence you inhabit by creating a pin. Would you like to create a pin?"

"Yes. 1119," It's Molly's birthday. November 19, 1986.

"Thank you. Your residence is locked."

Suddenly, I'm paranoid. "Lia can, uh, other people hear me when I talk to you?"

"No. Interactions with other players are sent via text message to help conceal your identities. Occasionally, voice messages may be sent using a voiceover technology."

"Lia, how do I get out of here?"

"I suggest the elevator."

A portal halfway down the shockingly dystopian hallway is illuminated. I walk to the elevator and select the down arrow.

"Say your floor number. For street level, say 'Street.'"

"Street." I say

The elevator descends quickly. Surreally. The doors open directly to the street. I step outside.

The street is moderately busy, peopled by women hauling laundry in wheeled baskets, men walking briskly, and a few children. Aside from the soft, ambient noise of the city though, no one is speaking.

I turn around. The elevator door looks like any other inconspicuous vestibule, and I wonder how I'll ever find this place again.

"Lia, how do I get around?" I ask.

"I can help with directions. Where would you like to go?"

"Red Lobster." I say.

"Red Lobster, great choice. Try Ultimate Endless Shrimp at Red Lobster for only $27.99. Sign up for My Red Lobster Rewards to eat, earn and repeat. I can give you walking directions to Red Lobster or call a cab. Walking will take you twenty minutes. A cab will take you to the restaurant instantly and costs just $20. Would you like to take a cab?"

"For two dollars?"

"Yes, the conversion is equivalent to $2 USD from your account."

I have just under two hours now.

"Okay yes I'll take the cab."

"That's great. I'll call Uber. Request Rides 24/7 with Uber, always the ride you want."

A car pulls up. I get inside. We drive for about eighteen seconds, which feels remarkably long when you're not *actually* driving.

Then there it is. Red Lobster. And there *he* is. Ahmed.

He's wearing a suit, which makes me smirk. It's a good thing he can't see my face. Or maybe he can.

"Lia, are my facial expressions translated through my avatar?"

"No. We use a combination of your biometrics and the inflection of your voice to render an appropriate facial expression and body posture."

Perfect. I do not have a poker face, a fact that's gotten me into a lot of trouble over the years.

I approach Ahmed. A window appears.

- A. Shake hands
- B. Kiss on the cheek
- C. Kiss on the lips
- D. Wave

What would Adrianna do?

"B." I say.

Suddenly I feel a hand on my hip and the soft warmth of skin grazing my face.

I jump. I almost fall out of my chair. It's so incredibly real. I can feel my heart pounding. My real heart. The blood vessels in my face dilate. I'm blushing. Hard.

Is that part real?

A dialogue box appears on the screen.

Hi. I'm Ahmed. Adrianna?

"Yes. It's nice to meet you." I say out loud.

Delivered.

Ahmed is speaking...

The ellipses roll on the screen.

Cool, I made a reservation. You look nice.

"Thank you. So do you."

You like the suit?

"I do." I don't.

Thought you would.

The Ahmed avatar winks. I wonder what his mission is. Maya said she died right? Or did she kill someone. Maybe he's going to kill me. Maybe this is my Jeffery Dahmer experience.

We walk inside and sit down. It smells amazing. Like garlic and butter and the sea. And suddenly I'm hungry.

The restaurant, like the street, is filled with ambient conversation and soft classical music.

"Have you been here before?" I ask.

Oh totally. We don't have many options in The Game. Not for date night, anyway.

"Oh really? What else is there?"

Mostly chains. Macaroni Grill. Taco Bell. Chipotle. They're the only ones who can afford sponsorship.

I'm relieved to learn that Ahmed doesn't believe that Red Lobster is the pinnacle of fine dining.

When I started, there were only two spots.

"What were they."

Guess.

"McDonalds."

That's one.

"Starbucks?"

Nope. KFC.

"No shit." I bite my tongue. Adrianna probably doesn't say 'no shit.' She's a classy lady. Stay in character, Alyssa.

KFC is really big outside the United States.

I wonder where Ahmed is from.

"Do you live in the United States?" I ask.

An error message appears on the screen. Then Lia's voice.

"Please refrain from asking questions that may inadvertently disqualify another player. Questions regarding their current geographical location, age, race or gender are not permitted."

I think back to the operating manual, the one that came with my headset. It was translated into at least fifty languages. Maybe Ahmed isn't even speaking English.

"Should we order?" I ask instead.

A menu fills the left half of my visual field. I decide, immediately, to order the most expensive thing on the menu, the Seafarer's Special. $38.95. It's half as much as my outfit, so I feel the expense is justified.

Ahmed orders shrimp scampi. His loss.

"Anything to drink?" the waitress asks.

"I'll have a martini." I say.

"Vodka or gin?"

I panic. There's nothing less cool than ordering a sexy drink and having no idea how you like it. God, I'm a poser.

"Vodka."

"How would you like it prepared?"

"Just," I pause, "The normal way." Worst answer. I look at Ahmed. His avatar's facial expression is neutral, but I'm sure behind the headset he (or she) is having a private laugh.

"And for you, sir." Our waitress turns to Ahmed.

I'll have a martini also. Gin, dirty, stirred, up. Bombay is fine.

"Wow. Fancy," I say. I'm blushing, again. I want to crumple.

You'll learn. With time. I actually don't drink outside of The Game. But I enjoy it here.

"Did you ever?" I ask, anticipating an error message.

A long pause. Ahmed is replying.

No.

The 'why' must have given away too much.

I'm guessing you don't either.

His avatar smirks.

"I'm more of a wine person," a half truth.

The whole truth? I'm white trash who couldn't tell a Malebec from a Cab if my life depended on it. I'd drink whiskey from a sneaker if it got me drunk.

I've also never had lobster before. I come from simple, midwestern folk. And to be perfectly honest, until I got to college, I too thought the Olive Garden could do no wrong.

The food materializes in front of us, and for five silent minutes—we eat. Just eat. We don't talk.

I realize that martinis are just vodka. Vodka olives. I shudder. The taste, however, is weirdly comforting as my body anticipates the sweet release. I'm lighter now.

The lobster, in contrast, is exquisite. It's other-worldly, soft and delicate. And even though I've never been to the east coast, I feel like I can taste the brine of the Atlantic ever so slightly on my tongue and in my sinuses.

I eat, and eat and eat and never get full. It's heaven.

Or maybe hell.

And in five minutes, the meal is gone. We've both cleaned our plates.

Was that your first meal in The Game?

"Yeah."

Not bad, eh?

"Not bad at all."

Another vodka martini?

Ahmed smiles. I've only taken the one sip. A first for me.

"No thank you."

Our waitress places the bill on the table.

My place?

He reaches for the bill. It's paid, and suddenly, the interaction feels slimy. Transactional.

It's just a game, I remind myself. You're not Adrianna.

But part of me is. And that's the crazy part. The line where Adrianna stops and Alyssa begins has gotten fatter, blurrier, murkier since the start of the night. We are like conjoined twins now.

It's just a game.

"You're not going to chop me up and put me in the walls?"

An error message. Lia's voice, "Players may not inquire about the nature of other players' missions."

I feel sick.

It's just a game.

"Your place," I agree.

CHAPTER SEVEN

Bells and Whistles

We get into an Uber, naturally. The clock is ticking.

I'm surprised to learn that we live at the same address.

"You live here too?" I ask excitedly.

Ahmed smiles.

We all live here. Most of us anyway.

"What do you mean?"

You live here until you reach a certain… pay grade.

I think back to the infinite rooms in the hallway where I live.

"How many people live here?"

The highest number I've seen is 19208.

"So there are 19 thousand of us? Playing, I mean."

At least. Probably more. Like I said, that's the highest I've seen.

Ahmed is laughing. I want to know how long he's been playing. My newness is such a source of amusement for him.

I wonder if he's fucking with me.

Ahmed pays for the Uber, and again, my stomach turns. What do I owe you, I wonder. Nothing in the whole world is free. And it's the unspoken tabs that are the most expensive. So what do I owe you for this?

We open the door from the street to the elevator.

221

The elevator stops at the second floor. We step into the hallway.

Ahmed pauses in front of his door, presumably to speak his pin. The door opens.

Ahmed's apartment, though in the same building, looks nothing like mine. His is nice. It looks like the apartments they turn into Zoom backgrounds with white walls and high ceilings. There are plants and mirrors and butcher block counters and one of those blenders my aunt has—a Vitamix. There's a white sheepskin rug on the floor in front of a leather couch. The fireplace is glowing.

And I know, I know, it's just a game. But I'm... impressed. I'm impressed by his fake things. By the trinkets he's managed to acquire.

I want to ask how he paid for all this. I want to know how long he's been playing. I want to know if he has a job.

These are tacky questions, though. I know that much. And I bite my tongue.

Can I get you a drink?

Ahmed walks to his refrigerator.

"Sure, whatever you're having."

He grabs two Modelos and hands me one.

"Thank you."

We sit down on his couch. He places a hand on my knee.

Tell me about yourself. I barely know you.

It's such an absurd question. I *barely* know how to answer.

"I'm pretty new here," I say, "As you know."

What else.

"Well that was the first time I'd had lobster. Just now. Maybe that says a lot."

He's waiting. Like a cat in tall grass, he's waiting.

But what can I say about myself that won't violate the rules? What holds outside of my age and race and gender? What else is there?

"I'm very loyal." I say. "I don't have many friends, and I don't trust most people."

That's smart. I respect that.

His hand slides further up my dress.

"Tell me about you."

A long pause.

Well, I've been playing for a long time. You could probably tell from my room number.

221. He's a founding father. This is George Washington.

"Have you ever died?"

Not yet. I'm lucky.

"Do you get older?"

Yes. When I started, my avatar was nine.

"What else? What else have you learned?"

His hand slides another centimeter up my thigh.

You start to learn that everyone has an agenda, yourself included. I don't trust anyone. But tonight I trust you.

"Why?"

Another centimeter.

Because you don't know how to play.

I'm excited now. I'm curious. I can feel my heart racing, the soft place in my lower abdomen rising and falling.

A message appears on the screen:

ENGAGE IN SEXUAL INTERCOURSE?

    A. Yes
    B. No

I wonder what would happen if I said no. I wonder if Ahmed had to initiate this window somehow.

"A," I say.

We stand up and walk to the bedroom.

It's more austere than I would have imagined. A bed, a dresser, a small lamp–not much different than mine.

I'm reminded of my mission.

"Kiss me."

I feel the heat of his breath, the press of lips, the tug of my own skin. My account jumps from $400 to $700–minus whatever I spent on this stupid outfit. And the cab.

"Thank you."

Do you have your controller in your hands?

"Yes."

Touch it. Anywhere.

I do. It begins to vibrate in my hands.

It's vibrating?

"Yes." I breathe.

Use it.

And all I can think of is, did I lock the fucking door.

***

It's ten p.m. A countdown timer pulls me out of bed with the urgency of an atomic bomb.

SHIFT ENDING IN FIVE... FOUR... THREE.. TWO.. ONE.

Darkness. I float in purgatory, the space between worlds. Then, finally, Lia's voice.

"Thank you for your work, Alyssa," Lia says. "Let's review the details of your mission to determine your compensation."

The mission appears in my visual field.

For this mission, your objective is to find a date for dinner. The date can be male or female but the dinner should be romantic in nature, ending with a kiss on the face or mouth. This mission is worth $300.

Receive a bonus of $200 if you secure a romantic date with a married individual. Receive a $400 bonus if the individual chooses to ask you out on a second date.

"You have successfully completed your mission, however it was not with a married man and the player has chosen not to call on you again. Your account balance is $692.73. How much would you like to cash out? Please remember that it's recommended to never cash out more than 50% of your earnings to remain competitive in The Game."

I feel a soft twinge of sadness and pain. Ahmed didn't really like me after all. He just wanted me to play with his handset.

Typical.

"I'll cash out $600.00," I decide. That's rent.

"Thank you, Alyssa. We'll see you next week."

Click. I'm free.

CHAPTER EIGHT

Take Two

The next morning, I call the women's shelter. I tell them I want to pick up a shift. But mostly, I want to talk to Maya.

"Well hmm, let's see," Christine considers, "I don't think Maya was expecting you til Sunday."

"Yeah I know. I just need to get these hours done," I pause, "And I really like volunteering."

"Maya won't be in til 11 this morning. Do you want to try and come by then? I can't promise she'll have work for you—"

"That's perfect." I hang up.

Debbie is thrilled that I'm "working ahead."

"That's the spirit, Alyss," she says, "I'm proud of you. Gettin' this stuff behind you and moving on. It's all you can do."

I feel the shame settle under my low ribs as I realize just how much Debbie wants me to turn my life around.

I know she just wants me to be happy. We just have very different ideas about what happiness looks like.

In my mother's mind, happiness is going to Home Goods on a Saturday morning and picking out a new candle. Or a plaque to hang on the wall, something that says, "But first, coffee."

It's getting to tell people what your oldest and middle child have been doing with their lives. How your older sister just had her second baby and your brother is getting married in June.

Happiness is making the centerpieces for the wedding yourself–insisting, in fact.

I know I sound condescending. I don't begrudge my mom these joys, but I don't want them for myself.

I think the trouble is with me that while I've always known what I didn't want, I never knew what I did. It's a disposition that has left me, well, suggestible, a trait that has only intensified with age.

It's the trait that landed me my first stick-and-poke tattoo, a lopsided popsicle on my left shin. But it's also why I started studying for the LSAT.

I literally had nothing better to do.

My openness to suggestion has been the start to countless adventures, ranging from brave to downright idiotic.

That's the thing about people: you can't just go cutting out bits and pieces without altering that person as a whole. Openness and suggestibility are the same trait—one just has a nicer name. It's the difference between mayonnaise and aioli.

This is something my mother has never been able to see. And my openness terrifies her. I think because it's something that sprung up on its own, outside of my conservative upbringing.

"Mom, have you ever had lobster?" I ask, buckling my seatbelt.

She thinks it over.

"You know. I think I must've at some point, but I can't for the life of me remember when."

"We should go sometime," I stare out the window.

My mom laughs.

"Seems like you're doing pretty well at your new job."

"The women's shelter? Did Darren say something?" A girl can dream.

"The remote thing. Or whatever it is. What is it?" She's understandably confused.

"It's like surveys and simulations. Stuff for big companies. You know like when Coke wants to see if a new flavor's going to land." I lie.

"There's a new Coke?" she perks up. We all have our vices.

"No, Mom. It's just an example."

"Seems like it pays pretty well."

"Yeah it does. I think I'm going to be able to keep my place."

A long pause.

"Alyss," she's being delicate, "I just don't know if that's the right move. You need accountability. The judge said you—"

"Mom, I know. You need to trust me."

"I'll talk to your father about it."

We pull up to the shelter, and for the first time, she drives away without personally witnessing me pass through the threshold.

It's 10:42. I pull out a cigarette and wait for Maya like a second-rate stalker.

God I hope she gets here early. The second we walk through those doors, I lose my chance to ask just about every question I have.

At 10:50, a green Accord rolls into the parking lot. The owner catches sight of me and rolls her eyes.

I wave.

"Well this feels a little like an ambush," Maya raises her eyebrows.

"I just really need to talk to you. I had my first shift yesterday."

She looks around nervously.

"You have five minutes."

I'll take it.

"So last night, I go on this date with a guy. And it feels like he's been playing for a really long time."

"What's the question."

"Well was he a real guy? Or was I like, you know, talking to a robot..."

"Most likely it was a real player. You can usually figure out the bots pretty fast. They ain't too bright, if you catch my drift. Usually they're placeholders–staff, waitresses."

"How many people are playing?"

"Thousands. Maybe millions now."

"Yeah this guy didn't seem like a bot. He was actually pretty nice. Helpful." I can sense I'm losing time, "Anyway, so he has this super nice apartment. Did he buy all that stuff?"

"Bought it or won it."

"Why though?"

"Why does anyone buy anything? Were you impressed when you saw it?"

"Yeah."

"There you go. Next."

"Okay so anyway, I'm supposed to get him to call me back, right? For the bonus. But he doesn't. And for the life of me I can't figure out why."

"Look, Alyssa. Everyone in the game has their own agenda. Sometimes they line up and sometimes they don't. You can't take these things personal. It'll get to your head. You gotta keep reminding yourself: it's not Alyssa this man rejected."

"Right. It's–"

She puts a hand up. "Uh uh honey. No thank you. I'm not trying to disclose this week. Got some good things going for me."

We walk towards the door. The conversation is over.

Christine buzzes us in.

I follow Maya down the hallway.

"And where do you think you're headed?" she asks.

"Oh," I say. "Christine mentioned you might–"

"No sir. I got my own list of to-do's today. Check with Darren. He might have something for you."

Maya can tell I'm hurt.

"Look honey. I know and you know that you didn't show up here to work. You showed up here because you had some questions. But I didn't plan nothin' for you today," she lowers her voice, "We gotta keep this stuff separate, you feel me? Look." She takes out her phone. "You can text me, okay? What's your cell?"

I give it to her.

"Be very careful what you put in writing. Matter of fact, call me. Don't text me at all."

I nod. "Okay. Thank you."

I meander to Darren's office at a subglacial pace. It's not that I don't want to see him–I do. But I need some time to rehearse. He's going to have questions, questions like, "Why didn't you ask Maya how to help?" and "Isn't today Thursday?" I'm not trying to look like an idiot.

But I can't very well say, "You know, I really just stopped by to chat with Maya about a secret game we're playing, but now I have to run down the clock 'til my mommy gets back."

Lying is like a game of chess. You have to stay three moves ahead of your opponent, anticipate their follow-up questions, be prepared to find evidence, and, most importantly, never implicate someone you don't trust. Unless, of course, they owe you a favor.

For this reason, I can't mention Maya, Christine or Debbie. My mother would never lie on my behalf. Out of principle.

I have to have my own alibi, my own reason for being here, and preferably one that makes me look good.

I ultimately decide to tell him that I'm not sure if I can come next week, but I don't want to get behind. Why? I have a dentist appointment, one that will conveniently be rescheduled. This will make me look responsible, proactive, and like I care about my oral hygiene. And I'll look even better next Wednesday when, against all odds, I arrive at my designated shift.

I knock.

"Come in," Darren answers.

I reach for the handle, but it's locked.

I hear footsteps hurry for the door. Click.

"Sorry about that," Darren smiles, "Hard to get anything done here without pretending I'm out."

I smile back, "I just wanted to let you know that I decided to come in today because I have a dentist appointment next Wednesday, and I don't want to get behind on my hours. I forgot to tell Maya, and she thought maybe you'd have something for me to work on."

The words roll off my tongue so easily.

The more lies you tell, the easier it gets—the less it becomes something that you *do* and the more it becomes something that you *are*.

I *am* a liar.
I *am* a smoker.
I *am* an alcoholic.

These aren't things that I do anymore, they're sewn into the lining of my skirt and written in expo marker on my soul.

"Thank you for being so proactive," Darren smiles.

"I like to be proactive about appointments. I know Maya goes out of her way to get ready for me. It's the least I can do."

Liar.

"That's incredibly considerate, Alyssa," Darren rubs his forehead, "God, I wish everyone would do that. You have no idea how many people show up here unannounced, scrambling for hours at the last minute."

"Well if it's harder to find something for me to do, I can always take an Uber home. No big deal."

"No I'm sure I can—" he looks around.

"Are you sure? I feel like this is just more work now—"

"No. You know what? I've been meaning to tidy up in here for months. Do you mind?"

I look around his office for the first time. The place is a mess. I'm actually not sure why I never noticed it before.

"Sure," I shrug.

In all honesty, cleaning Darren's office is my wet dream.

What he doesn't know is that I love to snoop.

"Thank you so much. You are a godsend, Alyssa, really. We really got lucky."

"Oh it's really nothing," I smile.

"I have a lunch meeting off campus. There are some cleaning supplies in the closet. Just, you know, make piles where you can," he laughs. Even his pigsty has become a charming character trait.

He leaves.

I start with the closet.

Three shelves, mostly office supplies. Also several Glade candles. Lilac. Gross.

There's a vacuum in the corner. Might need this, but it doesn't look easy to get out. It's behind a stack of books and sort of wedged under a broom.

A bucket on the floor holds what I can only assume to be the alleged "cleaning supplies," a roll of paper towels and a can of lysol.

I make a mental note to share this anecdote with my mother on the way home. Stories about men's incompetence as they muddle through tasks typically ascribed to women is one of her favorites. Seriously though–this is pathetic.

So far, the closet has been relatively tame. No skeletons to speak of, real or figurative.

The most logical course of action would be to put the room in order and then do my best to vacuum, wipe and dust. But if I do that, I might run out of time to rummage through the desk, the white whale.

Naturally, I set paper towels to the side and begin with the top left drawer. In my personal experience, this is the catch all drawer.

Pens. Highlighters. Post-its. Loose change. A pack of Camel Crush cigarettes. A bottle of Adderall. I pick this up. It's his name on the prescription. I guess it's kosher. I open the bottle and throw two in my pocket.

I *am* a thief.

What else… a few Starbursts. Trident. Two condoms.

Interesting, Darren. To be fair, he probably forgot they were there. He probably didn't anticipate that I'd be going through his desk. But who keeps condoms at work?

I place the Adderall back in the drawer, label face down, exactly as I found it. This is not my first rodeo.

The drawer on the right contains a few loose credit cards, more pens, more post-it notes. A thank you card.

Darren,

Thank you and your staff for providing me a safe place in my time of need. You truly are a knight in shining armor.

Love,
Maya

Maya? No shit.

For whatever reason, it's pretty hard for me to imagine Maya as a victim of domestic abuse. It's hard for me to imagine her as a victim of anything, actually. She's so tough and confident.

But what do I know?

I slide the drawer closed and get to work. I like Darren, so I really put my heart into it. I carefully straighten the piles of papers, the books and folders into neat little stacks. I set these to the side and spray off the surface of the desk, the computer monitor, and all the other non-porous surfaces. And in about an hour, it looks presentable.

I wonder how long it will stay this way.

I still have about twenty minutes to kill, so I decide to pay Christine a visit on the way out.

I let her know about my fake dentist appointment. She thanks me.

"I'll leave a note for Maya," she says.

The parking lot is empty so I decide to have a smoke while I wait.

"Mind if I bum one?"

I jump.

"Jesus."

Darren laughs. "Done early? You must work fast."

I hand him the pack.

"It wasn't as messy as you thought it was," another lie.

"Well thank you," he gestures to the cigarette, "And for this. I owe you one."

I smirk, "I wouldn't smoke a Camel Crush if you paid me."

It takes me all of a millionth of a second to realize my blunder. As the blood rushes to my face, we lock eyes. He knows.

"You saw those, huh?"

"Yeah. Just straightening up some loose pens and stuff."

Busted. I'm so busted.

Strangely, he doesn't look ruffled in the slightest. In fact, he looks—satisfied, a little mischievous, even.

"Find anything else?"

Uhm, yeah, condoms, stimulants, your credit card info…

"Oh you know," I take a drag, "Just the severed head of your last victim."

"How about the fake IDs? Do you know my real name?"

"If I do, am I next?"

"We'll see," he winks.

I shiver. He's too charming. He would be the *perfect* serial killer.

Darren laughs. Then, without warning, he reaches out and places two warm fingers on my neck.

"No," his hands smell like smoke and Dial, "I'd never cut a throat this pretty."

He drops the cigarette butt on the ground and walks towards the door. Christine buzzes him in.

I'm frozen. I'm speechless. I'm–

Fucking horny.

My mother pulls into the parking lot. I throw the cigarette on the ground, but it's too late. She's seen.

"Oh Alyssa," she shakes her head, "I thought you quit?"

"I did. I had. It's just really hard when I'm sober," I buckle in, "One thing at a time, you know?"

"I just hope Darren didn't see you."

"He didn't. I promise." Little does she know. "I *barely* smoke anymore, Mom."

She softens. "Well I'm proud of you for putting the extra time in. And for the new job, whatever it is. One foot in front of the other."

"Are you hungry?" I ask her.

"I suppose so."

"Take a left."

"Oh Alyss. We have food at the house–"

"Trust me. My treat. I just got paid."

She takes a left, and then another left.

"Here," I instruct her to pull in.

"Oh no, Alyssa. It's too much."

"We can split something."

She shakes her head, "Fine."

The waitress seats us right away. She sets the menu down, but I don't even need to look.

"One Seafarer's Special, please. We're splitting."

Debbie is skeptical. "And when was the last time *you* were here?"

"On a date. A while ago."

Our meal is presented with an elaborate flourish.

"Go ahead," I point to the lobster tail. We each take a delicate bite.

My mother smiles. "You know. I do remember when I had it last. Our anniversary dinner. The first one."

I smile too. It tastes *exactly* the same.

***

My second shift cannot come fast enough. Time really drags by when you're friendless, unemployed and broke.

The Game money, what I didn't spend on a lobster dinner, is spoken for. Rent, utilities, court fees, groceries. Sixteen hundred dollars really doesn't go all that far in this economy.

I consider getting a second job, but the idea of having to check the "felony" box kills me. I can't.

Besides, who would hire me? I certainly wouldn't. And how would I get there?

Before the accident, I was nannying a few days a week. It was a family I inherited from Molly when she got her "big girl" job.

"I guess I'll have to quit the Greene's," she mentioned casually, "Unless you want it."

"How much do they pay you?"

"Fifteen an hour. But Alyssa, it's so easy. The kid just watches TV and plays on his iPad."

She wasn't lying either. He was four. He loved baseball. Oh, and his parents were loaded.

What I didn't really expect was how much I'd love that fucking kid. His name was Garret, Garret Greene–Double G, Big G, Little G. And to him, I was just 'Lyssa.

The last time I was over there, he asked if I would play Monopoly with him. It was the kids' version, so not quite as tedious as a full game, but still a pain in my ass.

"Something else," I begged. Anything else. "What about we do the Wii for a little bit?"

"I hate Wii."

(He didn't.)

"Okay what about Candyland," I coaxed. Anything but Monopoly.

"Fine."

"Okay I'll get it set up and you brush your teeth."

He ran. I ran. I grabbed the game and flew to the kitchen table. I only had fifteen seconds, tops, to stack the deck.

All the good cards to the top of the pile. In order. This was going to be a ten minute game. At most.

"Ready," he sprinted around the corner, still frothing at the mouth.

"Wipe your mouth!" I laughed.

He wiped the excess foam on his pajama sleeve.

"Huh," Garret mused as his plastic avatar sped ahead to the gumdrop forest, "I guess I'm pretty good at this."

"You really are," I agree.

"Last time, Dad had to go all the way back to the beginning– right when he was going to win!"

"Amateur," I laugh.

"A what?"

"An amateur? It's someone who isn't good at something. Someone who's new."

"Yeah," Garret laughed. "I'm pretty good at this, huh? I play a lot."

"You are so good at it," I affirm him.

It's funny, you know, the stories we tell ourselves when we don't know the game is rigged. That we're good or that we're bad. That we just need to practice more. That we're just "unlucky."

Somehow we always pin it on ourselves. But most of the time, it has nothing to do with us, and everything to do with the game.

I never told the Greene's about the accident. I simply never showed up to their home again.

Mrs. Greene is one of my ghosts. I'm sure at some point she reached out to Molly, who texted my mom who told her everything. I'm sure she would have "had to let me go."

I always think it's crazy how you never know it's the "last time" something happens til after it's already over.

If I had known that was the last time I'd see little Garret Greene, I would've played Monopoly. Or I spy. Or whatever the heck he wanted. At the very least, I wouldn't have stacked the deck.

**

On Wednesday, I wake up with a sense of purpose. I make coffee. I clean the kitchen. I do my laundry. I shave my legs.

I even consider reading my text messages. It's too much.

But at least I don't want to die, which is a significant shift.

I double and triple check my headset and controller. They are charged and ready to go. And at seven p.m., so am I.

I place the headset securely on my head.

"Hello, Alyssa," Lia's pleasant, robotic voice sings.

"Hello Lia," I sing back.

"Are you ready for your second shift?"

"I sure am."

"I need a verbal—"

"Yes."

"Great."

Click. The headset locks.

I wait patiently for Lia to analyze my biometrics. I'm clean.

"Let's review your mission."

Subject: Mission Two

For this mission, your objective is to find a date for dinner. The date can be male or female but the dinner should be romantic in nature, ending with a kiss on the face or mouth. This mission is worth $300.

Receive a bonus of $200 if you secure a romantic date with a married individual. Receive a $400 bonus if the individual chooses to ask you out on a second date.

"Lia," I'm confused, "I think there's a mistake."

"I'm sorry, could you please rephrase your statement as a question?"

"It's the same mission as last time. Like, exactly the same."

"I'm sorry—"

"Lia, can you verify that this is the right mission?"

"Yes, this is the correct mission."

"Okay. Whatever."

I grab my phone off the nightstand. Three notifications, all from the Ember app.

This time, I'm going for the kill. Where are my married men?

Married men in dating apps all have the same profile: three faceless, shirtless bathroom selfies with a bio asking for "discretion."

To be honest, I've never really understood the appeal. But some girls go crazy for that shit.

Sal, 44, is here for a good time, not a long time. Kill me. His face has been conveniently left out of all his photos. Bingo. I swipe right.

It's a match!

ADRIANNA: Hi Sexy.

Send.

Sal is typing. That was fast.

SAL: Hi, Adrianna. How are you this evening?

ADRIANNA: I'm fantastic. How are you?

SAL: I'm golden.

Okay, Ponyboy. I roll my eyes.

SAL: But I'd be better if you were here.

Too. Easy. But it's not enough to get him to fuck me–I have to get him to call me tomorrow. He has to actually like me, to want me. What would Molly do? What would Adrianna do?

ADRIANNA: I'd be there in a heartbeat, but...

SAL: But what.

She'd make herself a commodity.

ADRIANNA: You have to promise me something.

SAL: Anything.

ADRIANNA: It has to be just tonight.

SAL: Sure.

ADRIANNA: I mean it. You can't contact me again.

SAL: You got it. I'm spoken for, so that won't be a problem.

ADRIANNA: Perfect. Where should we meet?

SAL: You can come over here. I'm room 1275.

ADRIANNA: Hmm I'm kind of hungry…

SAL: Let's order in.

I wonder if that counts.

"Lia," I ask, "If I have dinner with Sal at his place, does that still count?"

"Yes," Lia answers

ADRIANNA: It's a date.

But what to wear? I look in the mirror. Naked again. Do I start every shift naked, I wonder? Or only the ones after I…

I walk to the closet. What does one wear to seduce a married man? I have $100 in my account. Should I buy something new? A coat? Something less… prostitute chic?

Yes. I need to look–wholesome. I need to look like more than a good lay. I need to look like I make my own money. Thank god he isn't coming to my place.

I browse the list of stores, eventually picking out a floral sundress.

I wonder what season it is. Doesn't matter. I'm just walking down the hall.

Then it hits me.

"Lia, do any of these stores have pajamas?"

"Yes, here are a few options for pajamas."

A little silk set. Pink. Slippers. It's perfect. I'm just the girl next door, after all.

$107.89. But it's an investment, right? Right.

"Yes, that's fine. Make the purchase."

"Would you like to wear your purchase now?"

"Yes."

I indulge in a cursory glance in my mirror. This. This is it.

I emerge into the hallway and make my way to the elevator like an old pro.

"Floor twelve," I say.

The elevator departs. The doors slide open.

I walk to room 1275.

I take a deep breath. I wonder what my biometrics look like now.

I knock.

The door opens, but only halfway.

Hi.

"Uhm, hi. It's Adriana. From Ember."

The door opens fully.

Sal, 44, is, well, kind of homely.

He's about 5' 5" and a little rounder than his pictures let on. Maybe he's been playing longer than I have. Maybe you can get old and fat in The Game too.

I think he notices my hesitation.

It's just a game.

Sal is typing.

If you don't want to do this, it's totally up to you.

"It's fine. No, I mean–"

What do I say? It's cool that you catfished me? I'm here for the money?

"No, it's cool. No one looks exactly like their pictures."

I step inside the apartment. It looks like Ahmed's–but nicer. And a lot of the stuff is the same. Same subway tile backsplash. Same espresso maker. Same sheepskin accent rug.

Yours do. You look exactly like your pictures. Except you're wearing clothes.

I laugh. It's a fake laugh, the kind women use to make men feel comfortable. And Sal can't even hear me. I immediately feel like an idiot.

"Oh you could tell? It was my first shift."

Even in The Game, we all come into this world the same way.

"Naked and afraid?"

With an empty closet and not a dime to your name.

"Well I had a few dimes."

Respin money? So you must be smart.

"Come again?"

Well you get respins based on your IQ/EQ test. Didn't they tell you that?

"I guess they did. I didn't want to see my score."

Why not? I was dying to see mine.

A lack of self-confidence. No, don't say that.

"What does it matter? If you can't change it, better not fixate on it."

Sal walks to the bar cart. He uncorks a bottle of wine. He pours two tall glasses and hands me one.

To the wisdom to know the difference.

Sal raises his glass.

"Hmm?"

We cheers.

Nothing. You said you're hungry?

"I am."

Well, I have to say. The takeout options are slim here. Do you like pizza?

"I love pizza."

This is the truth. But who doesn't like pizza? And to be honest, I'd eat a ritz bitz sandwich if it meant the difference between $100 and $400.

Well, here's a test. Three toppings. Go.

He dials. A young woman picks up the phone. I panic.

"Pepperoni. Hot peppers. Uhh…"

Common you got this, kid.

"Pineapple."

Sal reluctantly repeats the order. He shakes his head.

There are two types of people in this world.

I laugh.

"No pineapple?"

I'll pick it off. Don't worry. We'll call it a practice round.

Sal winks. He takes a second sip of wine.

"Can I ask you something?"

Go.

"Do you live here with, well, your wife? Like do people live together in The Game?"

We do. She travels for her work.

"Oh."

I promise I'm not a bad guy.

"Oh I wasn't thinking that. None of this is real anyway. You might as well enjoy yourself."

Sal laughs.

That's one way of looking at it, sure.

The doorbell rings.

Your monstrosity has arrived.

He's funny. Genuinely funny. I can feel a familiar ache in my stomach. I want him to like me.

"Thank you for dinner. That was kind of you."

Thanks for making the house call. It's the least I could do.

He sets the pizza on the coffee table. It's from Pizza Hut, branded of course. He sets a plate down in front of me.

Dig in.

We each take a slice. Sal carefully picks the unholy fruit from his pie. I take a bite. Exquisite. I moan.

"Do you ever get tired of eating here?"

No. Not really. The food is and always will be perfect. It's like having a water dream.

"A what?"

A water dream. A dream where you drink something because your physical body, your material body is so thirsty. And it's perfect, but you're never really satisfied. You drink and drink and drink but you always want more. And eventually, you have to get up, drag your ass out of bed and go downstairs. You know, for the real thing.

"Unless you're smart."

Hmm?

"Well if you're smart, you stash the water under your bed before you go to sleep. And preferably a fruit punch Gatorade."

Sal smirks.

Fruit punch, eh? You're an old pro.

There is nothing I love more than a fruit punch Gatorade when I'm hungover. It is honey on my lips. I love it because it doesn't actually taste like any fruit known to man–it tastes like red. It tastes like sweet chemicals, like a mixture of cherry cough syrup and baby shampoo.

"What's your flavor?"

I'm more of a coconut water man myself.

So you're rich in real life, too. Okay, Sal.

"How many other people have you been here?"

Sal looks confused.

You mean how many times have I been reassigned? Well that's a personal question for a first date.

"Is this a date? I thought we were just hooking up."

You're right. I've been reassigned twice. Once because I disclosed and once because I died.

"You died? Tell me everything."

Sal looks uncomfortable. I've said something wrong.

"I'm sorry. I–"

Finally a message appears on the screen.

If it means anything, I wasn't scared to die in the real world til I died here.

I'm horrified. I want so badly to pry, so badly to know how–why.

"I'm sorry."

It's fine. And think of it this way. If I hadn't died, I wouldn't be here with you.

The silver lining, I suppose.

"Why do you say that?"

Well in my last life, I was a thirteen year old girl. So unless that's your thing...

"No. God no."

You'd be surprised.

And now it's my turn to squirm.

"I suppose everyone has their own agenda."

That's right.

I want to change the subject.

"What's the craziest experience you've had here?"

That's a good question. I mean, other than death itself? I think probably riding a horse. Have you ever ridden a horse?

"No."

I highly recommend it. If you can find one.

"Say more."

I guess I never knew how big they were. These things are huge. It's like driving a monster truck, but one with a mind of its own. I've never felt so powerful and vulnerable at the same time.

"You liked it?"

I was terrified.

"The whole time?"

Oh yeah. I never quite got the hang of it. Oh and the thing stepped on my foot.

"Did it hurt?"

Hell yes it hurt! Have you been hurt yet? It's only your second shift, right?

"Just during orientation. I stubbed my toe. Or Lia did. Actually, I'm not sure if it was my toe."

That's good. I mean I think it's inevitable. Part of the fun for whoever is watching.

"What do you mean?"

You didn't know?

"People are watching us? Now?"

Sure. I mean we're not doing anything particularly interesting right now. How do you think you get paid?

"I guess I figured it was all the strategically placed advertisements."

Well the endorsements are part of it for sure, but no–people can pay to watch. They can bet, too–send you on missions.

"Like puppeteers."

Look, if you have money on the table, you're not a puppeteer. You're a Player, just like us. And let me tell you, honey, the house always wins.

I look at the time. We have fifteen minutes left in our shifts. Or I do, at least.

"How long is your shift tonight?"

I have fifteen minutes. Same as you. Everyone starts and ends at the same time.

"I feel like I just got here."

Me too.

"I really like talking to you."

I do too.

"Too bad we'll never see each other again."

Well I guess we better make it count then.

Sal has a lot of charisma for a man of his stature. I can't help but wonder if he's handsome in real life, or if this bravado is simply derived from the fact that in ten minutes, we'll both be teleported to another dimension.

He stands up, leading me through the kitchen and into the hallway. He opens the bedroom door, his bedroom door.

Their bedroom door, I realize.

Her clothes are hanging in the closet. A bottle of perfume is sitting on the nightstand. It's branded, of course. Chanel No. 5. I pick it up to smell it. Glorious.

Sal locks the door.

"Are people watching us now?"

They could be. Does that bother you?

"Not at all. I kind of like it, actually."

This is not a lie. The thought of anyone watching my perfectly sculpted avatar's body engage in porn-perfect sex is, well, thrilling.

Sal begins to kiss the inside of my calf. He carefully, very carefully, sets my slippers on the floor next to the bed. Their bed.

Me too.

I wonder if he feels guilty at all. I wonder if you get attached to the people you marry in The Game, or if they're just—forms. I wonder if he was able to pick out the real bits of her. And if he could do the same with me.

Who was he kissing, after all? Adrianna's lips. Alyssa's soul. Who's thigh was he licking? It was attached to Adrianna, but it belonged to me.

Molly used to always tell me that short guys gave good head.

As the controller began to vibrate, I realized I was about to find out.

***

Our shift ended wrapped in wet sheets. The countdown warned us, but we said nothing.

I'm beckoned back to purgatory by Lia's familiar voice.

"Your dinner date, a married man, has left you a voicemail. As a result, you've received your full bonus. $600 has been added to your account.

Before you withdraw this evening, we have a special opportunity for you.

Both you and your date have been presented with an offer. If you make the same selection, you'll each receive an additional $1000 in bonuses this evening.

Both you and your date have received bonuses this evening. In order to participate, you'll need to wager these bonuses."

My heart races.

"What's the offer?" I ask.

"Would you like to pursue a long-term relationship with the player you connected with this evening?"

I'm sweating.

"Do I have to answer?"

"No. If you'd like to proceed to withdrawal, simply say, 'Proceed to withdrawal.'"

I am not a gambler. I think about my empty bank account.

"So $1600 total?"

"That's correct. $1600 if you and your date agree. Or, alternatively, $100 if you disagree."

I should take the $600 and run. I know this. I should proceed with the withdrawal and buy myself a full fridge of groceries. And I should put the rest in the savings account I'm always saying I'll start.

But I want Sal.

More than that, I want Sal to want me. I want to be wanted in this virtual world. Even in this silly game, I want to be the object of a man's desire.

It's mind-boggling, but I can't stop it.

"Yes." I spit it out.

"Please clarify your selection."

"Yes, I want to pursue a long term relationship with the, uh, other player."

So. Dumb. I'm so dumb.

"Thank you Alyssa. Please wait while your teammate makes their choice."

What seems like an eternity passes before–

"Congratulations Alyssa. You've been awarded $1600 for your shift tonight. Would you like to listen to your voicemail?"

"Sure." More than anything.

"Hi Adrianna. I had a really nice time with you tonight. And I know I promised to never speak to you again, but... What can I say. I never play by the rules. Plus, you left your slippers here, Cinderella. Call me if you want them back.

This is Sal, by the way. I guess you knew that.

Uh, bye."

It's the first time I've heard his voice. Or a render of his voice. Maybe it's the male version of Lia reading a voicemail he authored. But whatever it is, I'm melting. I'm crushing– hard. And I can't believe I have to live my own garbage life for a week before I can hear this voice again.

Of course, there's always Darren. But I get the sense that Darren is messing with me. I feel like a dormouse, small and dusty, quivering between his paws. How long will he toy with me, I wonder, before he bats me out of the way?

I don't want to leave.

"You currently have $1,700 in your account, including $100 residual, $100 base pay, and $1,800 in bonuses. How much would you like to withdraw? Remember, it's advised that you withdraw no more than 50%, as the money you earn can be used to gain advantage within The Game."

"I'll take out six hundred," I decide. Same as last week. Fewer questions from my mother.

"Thank you for playing, Alyssa. We'll see you next week."

Click.

CHAPTER NINE

Lo-Li-Ta

The time between shifts is almost unbearable. The contrast between my virtual reality and the hell I live in is comical.

In one life, I'm a bombshell who men leave their wives for. And in the other, I pay $87 a month to store a car I can't drive.

My parents tried to convince me to get rid of the car. To be fair, it was just about totaled.

"I'm not just *never* driving again," I told them, "Eventually I'll need a car."

"By the time you can drive again, you're going to want something reliable."

"It is reliable," I argued.

(It wasn't.)

Eventually they decided to drop it. I suppose they figured I'd run out of cash for the storage unit and have no other choice but to scrap what remained of Lolita. They made it infinitely clear that they *wouldn't* be financing this pathetic attempt to retain my dignity in the midst of utter chaos.

(My words, not theirs.)

I'm not an idiot. I know the car is a symbol. I know it represents autonomy lost. It doesn't take a psychology degree to figure that one out.

But knowing it didn't make it any easier to let her go.

Lolita.

Lo-li-ta. Named for Vladamir Nabakov's child bride, of course. Or his protagonist's.

It was my favorite book in high school. And so I named my first car after it–after her. Lo-li-ta.

When I bought her, she was twelve, pre-pubescent, though not in car years. She'd been a family's well-loved four-door sedan. Not exactly a babe magnet but well worth the $1,200 I paid for her.

I remember taking the city bus to the designated location, a Target parking lot. A middle-aged couple and their kid stood sheepishly next to the vehicle. She looked like the type of woman who wore a fanny pack to the airport, the kind that goes *under* your shirt.

She looked like her husband had to convince her that Craigslist was a reputable method to sell their beat-up old Corolla.

She looked relieved when a white girl in moon boots bounced off the bus.

"I'm Alyssa," I shook her hand. "You're Calvin and Mia?"

"Well no," not Calvin looked at his sneakers, "Those were fake names."

"For safety," not-Mia chimed in.

"I'm Dan. And this is Kelly."

"Oh," I nod, "I'm still Alyssa."

"We've never used Craigslist, actually. This will be our first sale," Dan shrugs.

"*If* she wants it," Kelly adds.

The kid tugs on his mom's wrist. She hands him her phone.

"Can I, uhm, drive it?" I ask.

The test drive was a formality. Unless there was a dead raccoon in the floor, I was buying the car. My dad had been poring through Craigslist ads for months. He even made a spreadsheet. This was definitely the one.

"$300 under Kelley Blue Book," he said proudly. "You can drive this thing into the ground." My dad had a knack for finding old shit. And by knack, I really mean obsession.

"Sure. I don't see why not," Dan smiled.

"Could we just see your license," Kelly interjected.

I handed her my driver's license. She nodded. Approved.

"We'll go with you," she says.

So we pile in, the four of us. Dan sits in the front, Kelly and the little guy in the back. She buckles him in with a feverish urgency.

"What's that smell?" I ask, turning the ignition.

"That's Rodney," the kid pipes up in the back seat.

Kelly rolls her eyes. I look at Dan.

"Our dog," he says.

"Potent," I smirk. "What kind of dog is Rodney?" I check the rearview mirror.

"Rodney gets car sick," the kid again. Gotta love them. Rookie mistake, Kel.

"He's a golden doodle," Dan answers the question. "We'll knock another hundred off the price."

To be honest, the smell barely bothers me. I've had dogs all my life. Nothing a little Febreeze won't cover up.

Once around the block, and I pull back into the parking lot.

"So what do you think?" Dan asks.

"She's perfect." I pull out my wad of cash. Kelly looks faint in the back seat.

"Good lord, did you ride the *bus* with that?"

I laugh. We sign the paperwork. Enter Lolita.

Two weeks later, that piece of shit was smoking on the side of the road.

When I took it to the shop, the guy told me the transmission was "shot," which I think is a word they reserve for women when they don't feel like explaining how to fix something.

My dad, feeling guilty, ended up footing the bill.

"Those assholes," he grumbled, "Selling a busted car to a young lady. Did they mention anything about the transmission?"

I shook my head.

"Dad, if they had, I would have said something right now."

"Dickwads," he handed his credit card to the mechanic.

That day I realized something. While my dad fumed, I was generally unaffected. It wasn't that I didn't think what Dan and Kelly did was wrong–it was. They *were* dickwads.

It was more that I'd come to grips with the fundamental truth that was causing my father's blood pressure to rise to medically unsafe levels.

This is it:

Most people, myself included, have an unsettling capacity to justify their actions. Most people can find a way to make themselves the hero of their own story. Most people *can't* tolerate being the villain.

Alternatively, it's a rare person who will admit they've done something wrong, that they've hurt you deeply, that they've caused you pain, even if that injury is permanent, irrevocable.

We compartmentalize and rationalize and then just stop thinking about whatever we did all together.

That's what Dan and Kelly did.

And although I hadn't done it yet, that's what I did too.

It's shitty, but it's true. And to be honest, if we didn't do it, half of us would probably end up killing ourselves.

Or maybe that's just me.

So as my father wrote his narrative, I forgave Dan and Kelly. Or rather, I let it go.

They were, after all, just trying to stay alive.

CHAPTER TEN

The More the Merrier

I wonder, often, if loneliness is the best kept secret in America.

When I was younger, really young, I used to list out my friends, for my bridal party of course.

I had it all planned out. There were six bridesmaids. Six best friends.

Over the years, those positions became vacant and were filled. People were promoted. Some left the company.

But the roster was always there, long after the day I decided I'd never get married, the roster was there.

See at a certain point, the entire concept of marriage started to feel incredibly dated to me.

Why promise your life? I don't know what I'll want in ten years–do you? If you think you do, you're crazy.

Ten years ago I wanted to be a high school teacher.

Five years ago I wanted to go to culinary school.

Two years ago I bought a book to study for the LSATs.

And today I just want to live in my own apartment and drive my own car to work.

I have no friends–just my parents and my two older siblings.

And the world does feel lonely.

The closest thing I have to friends are Darren, Christine and Maya. Maybe Sal, but Sal doesn't really know me.

Or maybe he knows me more than anyone.

My hours at the shelter are business as usual. Maya has made it infinitely clear what we can–and can't–talk about at work. And I respect that.

As for Darren, not a word since I cleaned out his office. I assume he's had a change of heart. After all, who would risk their entire career for a bit of young skin?

I do wonder if he thinks about me, notices that it's Wednesday.

Probably not.

So I clean out the freezer, wash the baseboards in the rec room, sort the kids' books, clear out the expired cans from the pantry. I do whatever's on my list, quietly and dutifully. I check in with Christine, she signs my form, and I leave.

And that's it–the highlight of my week, my solitary social engagement. I wonder if this is what it's like to live in a nursing home.

No, they have friends.

I consider getting a dog. Or a cat. A cat might fit the bill. Low maintenance.

But for a person who can barely maintain her own existence, the idea of a "dependent" is frightening.

Please, don't need me. I might not be around. I can hardly take care of myself.

Perhaps something less–sentient. A fish.

If a fish dies and no one is around–

No. I can't care for anything. Not a fish, not a turtle, not a succulent.

The only living thing in my apartment, aside from myself, can be a detritivore, an eater of dead things.

Feed off the bread I've forgotten, the yogurt in the back of the fridge. Thrive off my negligence. Ask me for nothing. Come and go as you please.

All I want is to play.

Wednesdays are becoming my favorite day of the week.

I used to look forward to Fridays–the day we'd most definitely go out. Now I thirst for Wednesday, Wednesday at seven.

I dream about the sweet *click* that marks the start of another dream.

My next few shifts are easy. My missions are unremarkable–silly even.

Decorate the living room.

Make friends with one neighbor.

Prepare a home-cooked meal.

The moments I share with Sal are easy too. It's like we've known each other for a thousand years.

I want to ask him about his "wife," the woman who was here before I was, but I bite my tongue.

Did he kill her? Was she reassigned? Or does she live next door now? Will I see her in the elevator on my way to Walmart? Will she ring me up at the Panera Bread when I pick up sourdough for dinner?

It's impossible to say. So like Dan and Kelly, I compartmentalize. *I* didn't cheat on anyone, after all. I'm just along for the ride.

I collect my allowance, $600 a week, and I wait patiently for my next directive in my perfect life.

And after ten shifts, I'm presented with yet another offer.

Click. The headset locks into place.

My biometrics are normal.

Before I read my mission, Lia says, "Congratulations, Alyssa. Today marks your 12th shift. You have officially been promoted to a level two player."

"Thank you," I'm not sure entirely what that entails. "Am I getting a raise?"

"No, you'll still be making your base rate of $25 US dollars per hour plus any bonuses you earn. However, you now have the opportunity to earn incentives for recruiting new players to The Game. Would you like to learn more?"

"Yes."

"Thank you. To recruit a player, you must simply receive verbal commitment indicating interest in The Game, as well as contact information. Contact information is generally an email address. This should be a personal account, not a work or school account, for confidentiality. If you're unable to obtain a personal email address, a personal cell phone number will suffice. Do you understand?"

"Yes."

"Thank you. While recruiting, we encourage you to share experiences you've had in The Game, however you must be careful not to give details that would allow the recruit to identify you should they agree to play. If you do inadvertently surrender your character's identity, you must disclose. Do you understand?"

"Yes," let's get to the money.

"For each player that you recruit, you'll be awarded a bonus of $500 USD. This will be deposited into your account once your recruit is onboarded."

I immediately think back to Maya's fresh manicure. I feel the sting of betrayal. No wonder she was so excited to have me sign on. I was a cash cow.

I shake my head.

Maya was just trying to help. I remind myself that this job is the *only* reason I can afford to eat—it's why I get to stay in my apartment. The Game is the best thing that's happened to me in a long time.

So what if she got a little bonus when I joined?

"Okay," I answer. "Is there, like, a limit to how many people I can bring on?"

"That's an excellent question. No, there is no limit to the number of recruits you can bring on board."

"What if the recruit quits?"

"All recruits are at will employees, like yourself. They may leave the company at any time per the terms in their contract. Their choice will not impact your bonus."

"Okay. I'm in."

"Thank you. To submit a recruit at any time, please use our secure portal. Access the portal via the text message you'll receive after your shift."

I cringe.

"Lia, can you, uhm, email me a link to the portal? I can't get texts on my phone."

"Certainly. Do you have any other questions surrounding recruitment?"

"No."

"Perfect. Let's review your mission."

For this mission, your objective is to secure employment. Receive an additional $1000 for securing a salaried position.

"What questions do you have?" Lia asks.

"Any job?"

"You may secure any position for which you receive a paycheck. This excludes under-the-table dealings and illegal activity."

"I can work at Taco Bell."

"Yes. What additional questions do you have?"

"I think I'm straight."

"Thank you. You will now have the opportunity to purchase credentials. You currently have $2380 USD in your account. Would you like to invest in a degree?"

"Uh, will that help me get a job?"

"It will help you qualify for certain positions, yes. Here are the degrees you can purchase. Keep in mind that for these purchases, your USD amount will have a spend rate of one hundred times its value."

A list appears on the screen.

Associates Degree from Community College - $10,000 or $100 USD

Culinary Arts Degree - $40,000 or $400 USD

Cosmetology Degree - $50,000 or $500 USD

Bachelor's Degree from State School - $64,000 or $640 USD

Bachelor's Degree from Ivy League School - $210,000 or $2010 USD

Masters Degree - $100,000 or $1000 USD

The list goes on…

I wish I could ask Sal what to do. He's had several chances to get it right, and based on the looks of his apartment, he's "invested" in a few degrees. But what do I know? He told me he works in finance, something about investments. Do you need a degree to work in finance? I mean, probably not.

You need a degree to meet the people who work in finance though. And you probably need a degree for them to take you seriously. I can't very well walk into Wells Fargo with my Taco Bell Employee of the Month Certificate, now can I?

Is "Finance" a salaried position?

Sometimes I feel so far removed from the world of the wealthy that I'd have to live twelve lives to get a seat at the table, and even then, it would be a folding chair, the one from the closet in the hall that's reserved for the unexpected extra guest.

I peek at my account balance again. To get the bonus, I need a bachelor's degree, I decide. That, or the Culinary Degree. That seems risky though. Especially in a world where Pizza Huts and Cheesecake Factories abound.

Ultimately I choose the State School. $640, gone. And I'm none the wiser for it.

"Choose your major," Lia instructs.

I consider it. I'd always wanted to be a teacher. That could be fun. A second shot, so to speak. Maybe my only shot, now that I'm a convicted felon.

"Education." I declare. There, that wasn't too hard.

A diploma manifests on the screen. I can't help but laugh. It only has my first name on it, Adrianna. I suppose no one in The Game has a last name. Still, it looks ridiculous.

"Congratulations, Adrianna. We've added your credentials to your resume. You may now choose three positions to interview for."

Ten spurious job postings appear on a laptop-like screen in front of me. It's Ember all over again, but this time with jobs.

What grade do I want? What subject?

Elementary science?

Kindergarten?

Middle school math?

No. I want to teach high school. I'm Megan Fox, after all. I'm going to be the *hot* teacher.

High School Art. That's the one.

I'm the hot art teacher, the one who you know smokes pot at home. The one who you think you saw walking out of the bar down the street from your house. That's me.

I select a few "safety" positions.

"Apply," I command.

"Thank you. Now submitting your applications. Please stand by while employers review your credentials."

I wait patiently for what feels like hours. In reality, it's five good minutes.

"Would you like to view a paid advertisement while you wait?"

Anything but this.

"Sure. Why not."

"I need a ver–"

"Yes. Play the ads."

You'd think by now, Lia and I would be speaking the same language.

I watch six or seven commercials for various products. The first one is for Endless Shrimp at Red Lobster. No surprise there. I can feel my mouth watering.

One of the ads is for a product I've never heard of, a new line of gluten-free frozen pizzas.

At the end of the ad, Lia asks, "Would you like to try a free sample of Freschetto Frozen Pizza?"

"Sure. Yes," I've learned my lesson.

A glistening slice of uncured pepperoni pizza shimmers into view. I can smell it. Then, *crunch*.

It's not bad. But then again, it's hard to mess up a pizza.

"Would you be willing to answer a few questions about the product? Your answers will remain confidential."

Again, I have nothing better to do.

"Yes."

"On a scale of one to ten…"

Lia delivers a series of questions.

"Wonderful, Alyssa. As a thank you, Freschetto has sent a five dollars off coupon to your inbox. We hope you'll try gluten-free Freschetto soon!"

Next, I watch a steamy cologne ad. Tom Ford. The entire headset fills with the thick scent of men's fragrance. I cough.

"Lia, this smells like garbage. Can we stop?" I feel my eyes stinging.

"The results from your applications are ready."

"Thank god," I hold my breath.

"You have been offered one position, High School Art Teacher at Sunnyside College Prep Academy. The salary is 65K a year. Would you like to accept this position?"

"Yes." I answer.

"Wonderful. We've added a 'Work' location to your Uber account. You can travel to work for free. Please note that when you travel to work, your avatar will be in uniform—no need to dress or change."

I wonder what the uniform looks like for an art teacher.

I feel like art teachers get away with wearing harem pants and long, flowing cardigans while the rest of the school has to walk around like business as usual. They're the types of teachers that let you eat lunch in their room so you don't have to sit by yourself in the cafeteria, the ones who play the Beatles in class and don't write you up for saying "shit," or "ass."

And they always have tattoos.

I feel a little warmth swell in my chest.

Pride. I'm proud of myself. It's not something I've felt in a long time.

And as soon as I feel it, as soon as my chin begins to lift from my chest, I stop.

This isn't my life.

This isn't my job.

This is just, just, *just* a game. I squeeze my eyes closed and remind myself. I click my heels three times.

This is not your home. You can't stay.

I trace the margin of the kitchen table, grounding myself in the material world. I clench my fists.

This is not your home. You can't stay.

The pride dissipates. I withdraw six hundred dollars from my account.

Click.

The next morning, I check my email. Just as Lia promised, a link to submit my recruits. And a five dollar coupon, which I add to my Apple Wallet immediately. Hey, a girl's gotta eat.

The only trouble with recruitment is my social circle has been, well, somewhat reduced. I certainly can't recruit Debbie. Or my father. Too many questions. Plus, I'd have to expose myself as a liar. Not a good look for someone who recently borrowed nearly seven grand.

I consider Molly. Molly would be the *perfect* candidate. Not to mention that it would be amazing to talk to *anyone* other than Maya.

There are a couple of other girls who work at the shelter. Kelsey and Diane. I met them in passing. Diane is in the same boat as me–court ordered. Kelsey is there because she wants to "give back."

I figure Diane is the best candidate, given her circumstances. Our shifts at the shelter overlap by an hour.

The following Sunday, I work through Maya's list with more fervor and intensity than I typically bring to the table. By the time Diane arrives, I'm all but through. I meander towards the front office.

Diane hangs her coat inside the closet.

"Hey girl," I sidle up to her. "What's on your list today?"

She pulls the folded list from her pocket and rolls her eyes, "I have to turn over room two. And it says 'wear gloves.'"

"Oh shit. Why?"

"Shit if I know," she stuffs her beanie in the sleeve of her jacket.

"You want help," I offer, casually I hope.

"Uh," Diane looks unsure. "Sure, I guess. What's your name again?"

"Alyssa," I smile, "You're Diane?"

"Yeah."

We walk up to two, gloves in hand.

I open the door, and the smell alone is enough to answer my question.

"I can't do this," Diane gags. "Nope."

She covers her mouth and steps out.

The room smells like a Goodwill, like someone had sex in a Goodwill. I crack the window. It's cold, but this is definitely the lesser of two evils.

I start by stripping the bed.

The sheets are stained with blood and—I don't know. I don't want to think about it. I hold my breath and stuff them in a trash bag.

The wastebasket is overflowing with used pads and yellowed gauze. I try and think back to who was in two. Grace. It was Grace's room. I wince, remembering her limp. This was probably why.

I feel the sting of tears in my eyes. I wipe my nose on the back of my sleeve.

Diane peeks through the door.

"I opened the window. Smell." I say.

She breathes in tentatively.

"Thank you," she rubs her eyes. "It was a rough morning."

"You look like you need a Gatorade," I hand her a pair of gloves.

"Something like that," She reaches into her purse, revealing a small, plastic bottle of Smirnoff Vodka. "You want some?" She takes a small sip.

I shouldn't, I really shouldn't. Actually, I haven't had a drink in a week.

"Absolutely," she smiles and hands me the bottle.

I wonder if she knows what I'm in for. She must. That or she's just in too deep to give a shit.

Bottom shelf vodka burns my throat. I shiver.

"This is absolute garbage," I choke.

"I'm on a budget," Diane laughs. She takes another pull from the bottle. "How many hours do you have left?"

"Too many," I sigh.

"What judge did you get?" she asks.

I consider, "I honestly have no idea. Why?"

"Probably Wyatt. I got Wyatt. Such a fucking asshole. Who gives him the right, you know? I'm just trying to get by, man. Fuck you."

I take a sip, smaller this time. "To Wyatt," I toast.

"To Wyatt. Rot in hell, ass fuck."

We start wiping down the hard surfaces. In spite of the smell, I'm enjoying myself. This is the closest I've come to camaraderie in months.

"You have a job?" I ask.

"Yeah. I'm part time at a blood bank."

"That pay pretty good?"

She smirks, "Not really. But they'll take anyone there. Why? You looking?"

"Maybe," I reach for the Windex.

"What about you?"

"I work remote," I say.

"Damn. How did you score that?"

"Maya actually hooked me up. It's one day a week."

Diane rolls her eyes. "That virtual reality thing?"

My heart drops. "Yeah. You play?"

"Nah man. Honestly, it sounds pretty suspect to me. $400 to sit around playing video games?"

"It's actually pretty cool. I made a grand last night."

Diane puts her hands on her hips. "And how'd you work that?"

"Well you get bonuses. Not every time. But like, a lot of the time."

"That's what Kelsey said too. I don't know."

"Kelsey plays?"I ask.

"Yeah. Her and Maya both. And you too, I guess."

"Who else?"

Diane gestures to the bed in room seven. "This girl said she's signing up as soon as she gets out."

Sounds like Maya's made the rounds.

"What happened to her anyway? The girl who was here. Grace."

Diane lowers her voice, "Husband beat the shit out of her."

"Did she have kids?"

"Not that she brought here. Not that I know."

I see Grace limp again in my mind. I wish I'd said something nice to her.

"She was barely here two months though," I continue. "Don't they get six? I mean why would she leave? Where did she even go?"

"I don't know. Probably back to him. That's where most of them go."

"Really?"

"Yeah, girl. You'd be surprised."

"Why? I mean whatever he did had to be pretty fucking bad. It smells like death in here."

"Old habits die hard," Diane shakes her head, "But I don't have to tell you that."

I look away, "Yeah."

"Look, no judgment. We all have our demons."

I can't stop thinking about Grace's small body, her dark eyes and soft red hair.

My phone vibrates. My mother's here.

"Shit, I have to go. Are you good with the rest of this?" It's not much now. "I can take the sheets down to the laundry on my way out."

Diane nods. "You're an angel, seriously."

"No worries."

"Hey let me know if you want me to hook you up at the blood bank."

"Thanks," I grab the trash bag and tie it off. Even so, the walk to the basement is tainted with the acrid smell of decay, flesh eaten off the body, wounds turned sour from neglect. I can't help myself. It's too much, and the vodka isn't helping. Tears begin to flow freely down my face, salty and black.

I catch sight of Darren and freeze. Too late. He's seen me. Crying. God I'm an ugly crier.

"Alyssa," he hurries towards me. "What's wrong?"

It's so concerned and genuine, which of course, only makes me cry harder. I drop the trash bag on the floor. I want to lie. I do not want to be vulnerable. But I can't think of anything.

"Where's Grace?" I sob.

"I wish I could tell you, Alyssa, but I can't. We need to protect her privacy."

"Did she go home?" Home feels like the wrong word. "Did she go back to him?"

Darren looks away. His eyes say everything. Yes. "What's important is that this place exists. And that the door is open."

I nod, but I'm still bawling, red-faced and ugly. He puts his arms around me and pulls me close to him. I succumb. I melt. I don't have the will or desire to be strong anymore.

I breathe his scent deep into the base of my lungs. Then pull away.

"What?" he asks, confused.

"Are you wearing Tom Ford?" I swallow the phlegm in the back of my throat. Disgusting.

Darren laughs. "Well. You really know your men's cologne," we lock eyes. "I take it you're a fan?"

Now I am.

I have an *intense* urge to kiss him. Every cell in my being is asking for it.

My phone vibrates in my pocket.

"Shit. My mom," I don't want to leave.

"Let me take this. You go," he gestures to the trash bag full of soiled linens. I reluctantly pull away. He squeezes my hand. "It's going to be okay. She'll be back, and we'll be here."

I nod.

"What on earth, Alyss?" Debbie sees my swollen eyelids.

"I don't want to talk about it." I press my cheek against the cool window.

Within an hour of walking in my door, I'm blacked out on box wine, the last of the stash.

Sometimes it's just too much to feel.

***

I wake up the next morning to two missed calls. Both Maya. Ten minutes apart. My unread text message notification number also seems to have grown by five. Not a good sign. My head is already pounding. I'm not ready for confrontation. It's too early.

Plus, I don't even know what I did.

I slip my phone under the pillow and attempt to go back to sleep. No luck. The pain in my frontal lobe is too much.

I drag my ass to the kitchen.

I pour myself a glass of water from the tap. It *tastes* like tap, overwhelmingly so. I contemplate walking to the corner store for provisions.

On the one hand, I feel like the walk alone might kill me. And who knows who I'll encounter in public.

But on the other hand, I need electrolytes. I need a Tylenol. I need this headache to go away.

I grab sunglasses on the way out the door. Incognito mode activated.

It's raining, of course, and I pull my hood up over my head. The cold water feels nice, actually. As I walk I utter an obligatory prayer to whatever God will hear me.

Take this pain away and I swear I'll be sober for a week. Or at least 'til next Friday.

I can smell the earth, wet and cool. The sidewalk is littered with earthworms. I do my best to avoid them, but not out of compassion, and not very successfully. Rather, I can't stand the thought of their jellied bodies on the bottom of my shoes.

When I was younger, I used to pick them up and move them, gently, to the grass. They were so fragile, so tender, their entire exterior as soft and delicate as the mucous membrane that lines your inner cheek, your eyelid, your private crevices.

Today, the heel of my combat boot haphazardly strikes a fleshy, segmented body, and I can't help but wonder what that little girl would think of me.

One thing's for certain: she wouldn't be impressed.

As I walk into the store, I take my hood down and make a beeline for the cold drinks.

Out of the corner of my eye, I see a familiar face, a familiar limp.

Grace.

I halt. I need to talk to her.

Is she alone?

I walk to the end of the aisle and peer around. By the looks of it, she's deciding between Log Cabin and store brand maple syrup.

I approach with caution.

I realize, as I'm walking past the pancake mix, that what I'm doing is against the rules and probably unethical, given Darren's comment about privacy.

But it's too late. I'm past the point of no return. She's seen me. She's recognized me. And now she's acknowledged me. A soft smile and a half wave.

"How's it going," not a real question, one asked rhetorically. She turns her back towards me and picks up a bottle of Mrs. Butterworth's Sugar Free.

This would be my cue to keep walking, but I can't.

"Grace," I smile. It's a forced smile. "Grace, right?"

"Yeah," she looks around. I'm making her uncomfortable.

"I just wanted to say…" What *did* I want to say? "I just wanted to say I'm sad you left."

"Yeah," she sets the syrup on the shelf.

"And I really hope you know that you deserve better," it's my last ditch attempt at executing my half-baked, ill-conceived plan. "And I think you should come back."

Grace shakes her head.

"I can't–"

"You totally can–" I interrupt.

"You don't get it–"

"Look, if you're embarrassed–"

"I'm not. I was having some issues," a pause, "With someone at the shelter."

A man pushes a cart around the corner.

"There you are," he places a hand on Grace's gently sloping shoulder. She flinches.

"Well nice talking to you," Grace smiles at me. They walk in the opposite direction.

I need to move, for Grace's sake I need to keep moving. But I can't. I'm frozen.

The entire walk home, her words echo in my brain. *I was having some issues with someone at the shelter.*

Maya? One of the other women? A volunteer?

I crack open the Gatorade and take the first sweet sip.

My phone is still under my pillow. Maya's called a third time. Now I'm ready to talk. Now I have my own set of questions. I hit redial.

"Bout damn time," Maya answers.

"I slept in," another half lie.

"Diane told me you been trying to recruit her–"

"Yeah, she said she was looking for some extra cash. I figured–"

"First off, I already talked to Diane. She's not interested. And if she changes her mind, she's still my recruit. Understood?"

"Yeah, whatever. She told me the same thing."

"And second, the shelter is off limits."

"To who."

"To you."

That's funny. "It didn't seem off limits a few weeks ago."

"Look. Feel free to recruit folks elsewhere. In fact, I encourage it. The more the merrier. But the shelter is mine. Are we clear?"

"So where am I supposed to find people, Maya? The gas station?"

"Not my problem."

"This doesn't really seem fair," I argue.

"Don't you have those AA meetings you have to go to?"

This stings, "Yeah."

"Try there. Bet they could use the extra cash. Of all people."

It's mean, a mean thing to say. And I haven't seen or felt Maya be mean before. Money really brings out the worst in people.

I weigh out my options. I don't want to be Maya's enemy. And if I cross her, my days at the shelter will be numbered. She's obviously close with Darren.

"Fine," I agree. The shelter is her turf. I can have the rag tag crew of alcoholics anonymous in my battalion.

"Great. I'll see you–"

I cut her off.

"Maya, why did Grace leave." A long pause.

"I suggest you mind your own on that one, honey."

Click.

The truth is, according to the terms of my probation, I should already be attending AA meetings. It's something I've been putting off. Mostly because I hate alcoholics, myself included. And between you and me, I have no intention of getting sober. It'd be fake of me to go, right?

The other thing is I haven't darkened the door of a church in over ten years. It's an atmosphere I'd prefer not to be in.

It's not that I don't believe in God. I do. But I don't think God's a "he." I don't think God has a gender at all. I don't think of God as a willed being, or even as a being.

I don't think God has arms or legs or hair. I don't believe that God is material or that he walked amongst us.

This alone immediately excludes me from just about every sect of Christianity.

I don't think God has desires. I don't believe he sees me or judges me. Or protects me. So that means Judaism and Islam are out. And that's assuming they'd take me.

When I was younger, I was both comforted and put off by the idea of an omniscient entity, one that not only stood sentinel while I walked to the car at 3 a.m. but also saw me ring my avocados up as bananas in the self checkout. 4011.

I was scared of the eternity of hell, but perplexed by the promise of heaven.

The answers adults were able to provide were riddled with dead ends and loopholes. Questioning, doubting, seemed to be a sin, a symptom of a lack of faith. This in and of itself seemed suspicious.

Systems that don't like questions are the ones we need to question most.

And as I got older, I did. I realized I would rather spend an eternity in hell than accept the half-baked answers, the bible verses used to prop up and sustain centuries of injustice, like toothpicks under a heavy quilt. How long could they hold?

After high school, I stopped going to church altogether. I was living in the dorms by then, and as mad as it made my parents, there wasn't much they could do about it.

Maybe mad is the wrong word.

Perhaps they were genuinely worried for my soul.

That makes two of us. But not because I'm worried about where I'll go when I die. That's the easy bit.

I'm worried that I'll never really get this life right.

So much of what I've spent chasing with all my heart seems so vapid and pointless in retrospect. I think of the hours and hours I've spent just trying to be *pretty*, the time I've spent trying to construct a version of myself that was easy to swallow, that made other people comfortable.

My Instagram feed is a self-contradicting paradox, a curated cocktail of body positive influencers painting glitter on their stretch marks and size zero models with noses made of silly putty.

And I still want those things. That's the worst part. I want the detox tea. I want the brazilian butt lift. I want eggplant emojis in my comment section.

Right now, a piece of me wants all those things, even though I know they won't make me feel full, even though I know they're water dreams.

Because if nothing else, they'll at least distract me for a moment from the fact that I don't know what joy or contentment or happiness are. I don't know how to be whole.

It makes me want to consume. It makes me want to swirl inside the vortex. It makes me want to throw up.

It makes me want to drink.

I don't think about God when I drink. Or my soul. Or my bank account. Or my DUIs or my medical bills or the cavity in my wisdom tooth or the dishes in the sink.

After three glasses of wine, there is no sorrow, no existential crisis. There is this very temporary freedom that accompanies being an id, a being that exists outside of time and therefor transcended worry.

It's not that the wine allows me to transcend time. That would be divine.

My favorite professor once said that it's our knowledge of time that makes us human.

No. This is more of a descension, I think.

***

The AA meeting closest to my apartment is at a non-denominational church, Christ the Redeemer.

I drag my feet on the walk. I feel like a con artist. I'm going to have to *befriend* someone. I'll have to be at least somewhat charming. I shake my head.

Networking has never been a strong suit of mine. *Networking* is code for disingenuous asskissing in the hopes of procuring a position of power. It's something fake people do so they can have one of those jobs that comes with a corporate credit card.

But hey, I steal avocados, so maybe don't take career advice from me.

Although I've never been in this particular church, it has a very familiar feel, a familiar smell to it. A sign on the door points the way. This group is called "First Step to Twelve." Clever.

I walk into what looks like a Sunday school classroom. A short-haired woman is setting up folding chairs in a small circle.

"Do you need help?" I ask. She turns around.

"Oh my goodness, you are early," she doesn't sound happy.

"I'm sorry. Doesn't it start at seven? The website said–"

"Seven thirty," she answers, "Hasn't been seven for months now."

"Oh," I'm about ready to leave at this point.

"Well grab a cup of coffee then," she points to an urn.

To my utter relief, she leaves the room, who knows for how long. I do as I'm told and grab a cup of coffee, even though it's seven and I know it's too late. I'll be up all night. That's fine.

It's watery and piping hot and strangely nostalgic. This is exactly how my dad likes his coffee.

If you asked him, he'd tell you he likes a dark roast. He doesn't. People have no idea what they really like. We're all just brainwashed to parrot what we think is desirable.

I like blondes. I like muscles. I like goldendoodles. I like granite counters.

No one says they like watery store brand coffee. Maybe if just one person was brave enough, or self-aware enough to admit it, other people could say it too.

I think if we all had permission to shamelessly explore our true desires, we'd all be a little more connected and a little less sad.

But again, I'm very sad, so maybe don't take interpersonal advice from me.

I sip my coffee and scroll through old photos on my phone. I wish I had my headphones. Anything to hide behind.

I remind myself that one does not make friends with headphones in. I'm supposed to look *approachable*.

I put my phone in my backpack and attempt a breathing technique a therapist taught me once.

In to the count of four. Hold at the top. Out to the count of six. Hold at the bottom.

I think it was called "box" breathing. It works, strangely enough. If you can concentrate long enough to build a few boxes. Often I can't.

Today is one of those days.

I check my watch. 7:12.

In to the count of four.

Can one box breathe for twenty two minutes?

Hold at the top.

As it turns out, I don't need to find out. A man in bike shorts clambers in, winded. He's carrying a road bike, the kind without a kickstand. Okay cool guy.

"Hey," he says.

"Hi," I size him up for potential recruitment. He looks healthy and like he has the will to live. We do not belong to the same genre.

"I'm Brendan," he extends a hand.

"Alyssa," it's a weak handshake, the kind where the grip isn't quite right but you're, you know, already shaking.

"Good to meet you. I don't think I've seen you here before."

"It's my first time," I confess.

He nods, "Groovy."

Oof. There is a certain brand of people that can hold their own in spite of comments that make you cringe. I am not cut from that cloth. I have no poker face. "Groovy" hits me like a sip of milk when you thought you were getting Diet Coke.

I sit back down. Brendan doesn't take the hint.

I suppose I should be grateful. Someone to talk to. But I'm not.

"I really like this meeting. One of the better ones."

"Mm," I nod.

"It's all about the people. If people are gonna be real, you know. Enough bullshitting. You gotta be real if you want to be sober."

I take a sip of coffee. I consider pulling out my phone.

When Molly and I used to go out, we developed a system for telling a guy you're not interested without, you know, *actually* telling him.

Pulling out your phone is level two.

Looking back, it's pretty messed up that I never felt empowered enough to just say, "Hey man, I'm not super interested in talking to you." But if you say that, you're a bitch. Nice girls don't use their words; nice girls use a cleverly devised system of non-verbal cues that make other people comfortable. Nice girls are passive.

Level one. Don't contribute to the conversation. Smile and nod. Be polite. But don't ask any questions. And don't give particularly thoughtful answers.

Level two. Take your phone out. You'd be surprised how well this works. If the person you're speaking to has any type of social intelligence, that is. Very very few people are willing to stand there while you text your mom to make sure the dogs get their heartworm pills.

Level three. Take or make a call.

The door opens. Thank God. Praise Jesus. Hare Krishna. Another person. But not just any person.

"Alyssa?" Darren spots me. I nearly jump out of my seat. Not very suave, Alyssa.

"Hi!"

Tone it down.

"Hey," I lower my voice an octave.

Brendan meanders towards the coffee. Talk to another man is level six. But if you have to escalate to six, he kind of deserves it.

"I'm glad to see you here," Darren takes the vacant folding chair to my left.

I blush. "You saw my file, huh?"

"Your mother told me, actually."

Of course she did.

"No judgment," Darren smiles. "I'm here too."

I nod, "Right."

Unlike Brendan, Darren is attune to my body language. "You look nervous."

"It's my first time here. I don't know what to do with myself. And I feel–kind of fake."

I don't know why I'm being this honest.

He smiles, "Everyone feels that way."

I wring my hands, "So are you like, my sponsor now?"

Darren laughs, "I guess I could be. Why don't you get through your first meeting first?"

And I do, I survive my first meeting, "Hi I'm Alyssa" and all.

I pack up my chair and place it neatly on the rack.

"Coffee?" Darren asks. It's so casual, so smooth. I almost forget why I came here.

"I had some, thanks."

He laughs, "Not this. I meant do you want to get a coffee?"

I do. More than anything.

"Sure." No recruits today.

"Denny's?" he asks.

"Oh. I walked here."

Another laugh, natural and warm. "I can drive. I drove."

We finish racking the chairs and walk out to the church parking lot.

I guess, in spite of his office, I always imagined Darren with a nice car. This is not that. This is a fifteen year old Toyota.

He tosses an empty fountain drink off the passenger seat.

"Madame," he ushers me in.

We're seated at a booth, cracked in a few spots. The restaurant is mainly empty, aside from a few college kids freeloading in a corner.

"Coffee?" the waitress asks.

"Yes please," I push my mug toward her.

"And a round of pancakes," Darren adds, "For the table."

It's cute. The right kind of cute. I feel like I'm in a movie.

"So you want a sponsor," he leans forward.

"I guess," I swallow. I don't want a sponsor. But I do want to be here. I want his eyes on me. I want his attention. "Sure."

"Not very convincing, Alyssa."

He uses my name a lot. I've heard this is a trick, that we like people who say our name. I like hearing him say my name.

"I do want a sponsor," I need to sound more sincere, "I need more accountability."

"Say more about that."

Our waitress sets a stack of pancakes on the table.

"I mean," I fumble, "I don't really have a reason to stop drinking at this point. I know that sounds selfish."

"It is a little selfish."

"I know." Oh trust me, I know.

"But one thing I've learned, and this is important," he pauses, "Is that this disease, alcoholism, it makes people selfish. And not the other way around."

"What do you mean?"

"Well I think a lot of people feel like selfishness is the root of their addiction. And really, addiction is the root of selfishness."

I still don't follow, "I'm sorry?"

"You think that you're a bad person, and that's why you drink. But in reality, drinking makes you a bad person."

This is news to me. "I don't know, Darren. It's pretty fucked up to drink and drive."

"It is. That's true."

"Like," I can feel myself about to cry, "*Really* fucked up."

He looks me in the eye. "You have a deep soul, Alyssa."

Too deep, I think. *Bottomless. A void.*

"Can you swim?" I ask.

"I'll try," he smiles, "Although, I probably shouldn't even be here."

"Why not?"

"Oh you know. The fact that you work for me. The fact that I sign paperwork for you. The whole power dynamic thing."

He rolls his eyes when he says "power dynamic," as if it's something silly, trivial.

"I mean," I smile, "You don't cut my paycheck. There's that at least."

"The fact that I'm older than you. The fact that I know your mother."

"Debbie? She loves you."

"The fact," he continues, "That I'm intensely attracted to you–it's a recipe for disaster."

I inhale sharply.

"The fact that I want to drown in your soul," he shakes his head.

I feel my heart pounding.

"So you won't be my sponsor," I ask, mostly to cut the tension.

"I'm not saying that. I'm saying I *shouldn't* be your sponsor."

"What if we're just friends?"

He slides down the booth. "We could be friends. That would be better."

"I could use a friend right now," it's the truest thing I've said all day.

A hand slides up my thigh.

"I can be a friend."

I can feel my breath quickening, those autonomic short breaths, breaths that ready you for–

"Do you want to come over?" he asks.

I nod. More than anything. I want to come over.

Darren lives on the west side of town. He parks his car on the side of the road. It's a multi-unit situation, which is pretty normal for this side of town, but not so normal for a guy his age.

"Do you have roommates?" I ask.

"No, thank god," he smiles. "Just me."

We walk up three flights of stairs. No elevator. I'm winded.

The apartment is sparsely decorated. A sad-looking houseplant. A synthetically-upholstered futon. A Phish poster. A record player.

"What do you listen to?" he asks.

"Beach House?" I ask.

"Try again," he smiles.

"You pick," no need to embarrass the man.

He pulls out an old Bright Eyes album.

"Ohhhh, you're sad, huh?" I smile, maybe the first real smile of the night.

He sits down next to me on the futon.

"Oh, very sad," he swings my legs over his lap.

There is something so lovely about sharing misery with another person.

He tilts my head gently towards his.

Lips on lips. A hand that makes its way under my skirt and deep between my legs.

And so we swam. My soul in his and his in mine.

CHAPTER ELEVEN

Sleeping on the Job

I start attending meetings pretty regularly, not just "First Step to Twelve," but others as well.

On Saturdays, I go to "Sober Sisters." This is an all girls group.

On Fridays, I hit up "LGBTQs for Sobriety."

And on Monday mornings, I go to "Morning Sippers."

And eventually, with a little gumption and perseverance, I befriend a chubby blonde girl named Claire.

Claire goes to Sober Sisters. She works a desk job, which explains the curvature in her spine and the shape of her torso. She's gluten free and dairy free. And an alcoholic.

The first time I notice her, she's inspecting the nutrition label on the Coffee Mate bottle. It's French vanilla.

"Do you think this is gluten free?" she asks me.

I push the half-and-half toward her. "I'm not sure, but this is."

She spins the carton around. "Got a lot of fat in it," she frowns, "Plus I'm dairy-free too."

"I'm Alyssa," I say.

"Claire," she picks the Coffee Mate back up. "Nine grams of sugar. Is that a lot?"

"I don't really know. Yeah?" I say.

"Oh well," she sighs, "I did a spin class before this."

We sit down next to each other.

"I've never done a spin class," I offer. My mother says it's best to connect with someone over something they're interested in. I'll give it a go. "Do you like them?"

"I love them," Claire lights up. Bingo. "I go to Infinity Spin on the east side. Do you work out?"

I don't but, "Yeah sometimes."

"Yoga? You look like you do yoga."

I wonder what about me exactly says yoga. I guess it doesn't matter. "Uh huh," I nod.

"Where do you practice? I used to go to the place over by the mall. What's it called?"

I have no idea, "Uh I mostly just do it at home. Like online."

She nods, "Yeah that place closed anyway. Probably because it was so expensive. At home is the way to go. Who has $25 for a sixty minute class? Plus you don't even burn that many calories." She pauses, "No offense. You look like you're in great shape."

I'm wearing a Sublime hoodie and leggings. My shape is swallowed by folds on folds of tie die fabric. "Thanks," I say, "So do you."

Claire smiles, "I've lost six pounds since I got sober. It's like half the reason I'm here."

"Wow, that's amazing," I force a smile.

"We should do spin sometime," she sips her coffee.

I guess this means I'm in. "That sounds good," I agree.

After the meeting, we walk out to the parking lot.

"Where did you park?"

"I walked here," I answer, "Gotta get those steps in."

Claire looks at her fit bit and rolls her eyes. "I know. Maybe I'll go to the gym."

"Should we exchange numbers?" I ask.

"Yeah. I'm kind of a shitty texter," she admits. "But call me. Whenever."

Even better.

I dial her number. Her phone rings.

"Got it. Alyssa, right? A-l-y-s-s-a," she adds my contact into her phone. "There. Alyssa Sober Sister."

I wait til Tuesday to call. Trying to play it cool, or whatever.

"Hey girl," she answers, "What's up?"

"Just wanted to see what you're up to tonight. Like after work."

"Well I'm definitely going to cycle. There's a spin class at six thirty. Should I sign you up?"

I consider the fact that I'll have to Uber there and back. And pay for the class.

"How much is it?" I ask.

"It's $10 your first time. But you'll definitely want to become a member. Trust me. You're gonna be hooked."

I seriously doubt that.

"Okay. Infinity Cycle, right?"

"Yep, six thirty."

Click.

At five thirty, I order a $22 Uber to drag me across town in rush hour traffic. I'll write it off as a business expense. If she signs up to play, it'll be worth it.

So far, it feels like a gamble. Claire doesn't seem like the type of a girl who's looking to work a second job. She has a membership at at least one gym and one boutique fitness studio. And she doesn't eat gluten or dairy.

I walk into Infinity Cycle just as the class is about to start.

"There she is," Claire waves at me. "We're on ten and eleven." She looks at my outfit disapprovingly. "Converse really aren't the best shoes to bike in, but it's fine."

Spin class is my nightmare. The room is entirely dark. House music blares as the instructor shouts into her headset.

"You came here to work! Let's dial it up."

It feels like I'm in a club, but there's no alcohol. And I'm also working out. It's like a very niche version of hell.

Finally it's over.

"Should we grab dinner?" I ask.

"Why not," Claire answers, "We earned it."

This sounds like something my mom would say.

"Do you have any favorites?"

"There's a salad spot around the corner. Do you like salad?"

"Sure."

It's a build-your-own salad situation. "First you pick a base," Claire instructs me, "I like spinach and mixed greens. You can pick whatever you want."

We slide down towards the salad dressings.

"None for me," Claire says proudly.

This bitch is about to eat a dry-ass pile of leaves. Nope.

"Do you have ranch?" I ask.

"We have a greek yogurt ranch," the woman behind the sneeze guard informs me.

"It's good," Claire approves.

"Okay," we arrive at the cashier–end of the line.

"$16.34," the cashier announces.

"I'm getting hers too," Claire gestures to me.

"You don't have to–"

"It was my idea. You can get next time."

We slide into a booth. Claire watches me take my first bite like a parent introducing their two year old to the Lion King.

"It's good. Thank you."

"I know. They have the best salads. I come here like three times a week."

I do the math. This woman is spending $50 plus dollars a week on salads alone. Her potential for The Game is not looking good.

"So what do you do for work?" I ask.

"Oh I'm an administrative assistant. Basically a secretary."

"That's cool. Do you like it?"

"I don't mind it. It pays pretty good."

"That always helps."

"I mean," she pops a cherry tomato into her mouth, "I still have *mounds* of credit card debt."

"Really," my interest is piqued, and I immediately feel guilty. What kind of a sick person gets excited when someone tells them about a crippling financial obligation?

"Yeah but," she laughs nervously, "Who doesn't?"

"Yeah. Have you ever thought about maybe getting a second job?"

Claire looks exasperated, "I mean of course. But I don't have time. I work out every day after work. I mean, I could do something on the weekends but. I don't know. It feels kind of embarrassing to have two jobs after thirty. Don't you think?"

No, I think to myself, *what's embarrassing is having no jobs after you're thirty.*

"Yeah," I say out loud, "I get what you mean."

"What do you do?" she asks me.

"Oh I work remote," I say casually, "It's super chill and I only have to work one night a week."

"Shut up," Claire's eyes get wide, "How are you paying your rent? You must own your house."

This time I laugh right out loud. It's too much. "Girl no. I definitely do not own a house. I don't even have a car."

Claire nods, then becomes suddenly suspicious.

She narrows her eyes and lowers her voice. "Alyssa," she leans towards me, "Are you a *cam girl?*"

"No! No. Nothing like that at all. It's like," I pause. I should have rehearsed this. "Well it's like a game I play. But along the way I have to watch ads and rate products and stuff."

"So like," she considers, "Market research."

"Sort of. Yes."

"Well are they hiring?"

It's almost too easy.

"Oh definitely," I say. "They're always hiring."

"How much are you making?"

"Like $400 a night."

"Do you think you could get me in?"

I smile. If I was a cartoon villain, you'd see dollar signs in my pupils.

"Oh definitely. It's the least I can do."

"That would be amazing."

Claire scrawls her email address onto a napkin. She looks down. Is she crying?

"What's wrong?" I ask.

"Honestly," Claire sniffs, "Things have just been pretty shitty lately." A pause, and then, "I'm just really lucky I met you."

And so, Claire becomes my very first recruit.

I enter her name and email into the system that very night. Two days later, my recruitment check hits my bank account. She's tasted the lemon. She's stubbed her virtual toe. She's signed the paperwork.

The following Saturday, we walk together from Sober Sisters to a cafe on the corner. Claire is itching to talk.

"How was it?" I ask excitedly.

"That headset is wild," her eyes widen. "All I want to do is eat."

I laugh. I know the feeling. Claire is starting to feel like a real friend. And for a moment, that makes me happy. I consider telling her about the bonus.

No. It's too late. She'll find out eventually.

She sips her sugar-free soy milk latte and asks many of the same questions I attempted to pry from Maya. I tell her as much as I can, and again, she thanks me.

Over the next few weeks, I'm able to recruit three more girls.

It's nice, at first, but as the months go by, my shifts get weirder and weirder.

It feels strange to be living with Sal. Every shift starts together in our (his) beautiful house. Sometimes he makes me coffee. Sometimes we just fuck.

Most mornings, we share our missions. This is fine, Lia informs me, so long as the mission doesn't directly involve him.

I look forward to seeing him. He feels like a partner. He offers me tips for recruiting. Apparently he's recruited over a hundred people. He teaches me how to spot a bot.

But I also feel like I'm cheating on Darren. I realize that this is only half true. Besides, Darren isn't my boyfriend. But the closer I get with Darren, the cheaper the seven minutes of pleasure I share with Sal starts to feel.

Eventually, this part of our relationship is phased out. And it's around this time that my missions start to turn.

It's hard to explain it, but it almost feels like someone's trying to fuck with me.

I tell myself I'm paranoid. But maybe I'm not.

Today, your mission is to leave work early.

Today, your mission is to get out of a speeding ticket.

Today, your mission is to get a colleague fired.

"Do you think I should do it?" I ask Sal at the breakfast table.

There's a long pause. He sips his Starbucks Single Origin dark roast.

I don't know. If I'm being honest, I would.

"Really? It just feels kind of–wrong. Is it wrong?"

It's just a game, Adrianna. Someone's going to win. It may as well be you, right?

"Maybe," I'm not convinced.

Does that make me a bad person?

"I don't know. Is it possible to be a bad person? Isn't the goal to win the game?"

I suppose. Look. I can at least tell you that getting someone fired would not be the worst thing I've ever done in The Game. Not by a long shot.

"What's the worst?"

You don't want to know. Trust me.

I want to know more than anything. I'm Brad Pitt in *Seven*. I need to open the box.

"Tell me. After all. It's just a game, like you said."

You remember how I was married when we met?

"Yes." This feels like an eternity ago. But in reality, it's only been a few months.

Well, in order to be with you, I had to leave my wife, obviously.

"I mean yeah, that makes sense."

I had to kill her.

My stomach drops.

"How?"

Oh, I could choose any number of ways. But the sick thing is—

A long pause.

The sick thing is that some of the, uh, methods... some of them had higher dollar amounts.

"What do you mean? Like your bonus?"

Yeah.

I think about the searing pain I felt from simply stubbing my toe. And I know, I *know* I shouldn't ask the next question. But I can't help myself. The box is open. I can't stop.

"What did you choose?"

I feel nauseous.

Adrianna...

"Just tell me. It's not real."

Fire.

"You burnt her? Like... Like a fucking witch?"

I mean. No. I selected an option in which the building she was in burnt to the ground.

"Did she know it was you?"

I'm not sure. I think if you play long enough, you generally assume that anything bad that happens to you is because someone else chose a bonus. There are no acts of god here.

I'm appalled.

"Did you feel bad? Like at all?"

I really needed the money.

"God."

SAL: Yeah. So getting someone fired? Playschool stuff. I wouldn't think twice.

I consider it. Sal's been playing for a long time. I wonder how long it was before he killed another player. I wonder if they're just warming me up.

"So how do I do it?"

Look, the game isn't infinite. You'll probably be given some options when you get to work.

And he's right. When I walk into my classroom, I'm greeted by Mrs. Stein, 67. She teaches chemistry. Definitely not a bot.

I've had one or two interactions with her. She seems kind. She seems like the kind of teacher you'd want in real life.

Please, please let it not be Mrs. Stein, I think to myself, *Anyone else.*

But of course, it's no coincidence. Mrs. Stein is a pawn. Whether she knows it or not is beyond me. I wonder what her mission is today. I wonder if it's her or me. I wonder if the real Mrs. Stein is a fifty-six year old pedo.

There is no real Mrs. Stein. Just like there is no real Adrianna.

I place a bottle of Oxy in her top drawer. I could have planted a gun or a student's nude photo.

As I slip the pills between the neatly arranged office supplies, I stash a single pill in my pocket.

I wonder…

I place the pill on my tongue and crush it with my teeth. I swallow.

Yes. Oh yes. It works here too.

***

The second my headset clicks, the high is over.

I smile. No hangover. Nice. Then I remember Mrs. Stein.

It's just a game.

I need to talk to Maya. Or Claire. Though, if Claire had been asked to burn someone at the stake, I can only assume she'd have gotten in touch with me.

"What's good, honey," Maya picks up the phone.

"Maya have you ever killed someone? In The Game."

"Once. Yes."

"And you said you've died, right?"

"Yes."

"Do you think someone else did it?"

"I do."

"What did it feel like to die?"

"Dying wasn't nothing. It was getting there that was hell. Then I just blacked out. Woke up at the end of my shift when the headset unlocked."

"How did you die?"

"Car accident."

"And how did–"

"I think it's best you just let it come. If you're going to take anything from this, it's that nobody is your friend, not in *The Game*. Nobody. You might think they're your friend, that y'all teamed up. Think again. Everyone is playing. There are no teams."

"Okay."

"At the end of the day, I advise you to treat this like a job. Get in. Get out. Get paid. Leave your feelings at the door."

"Okay. Thanks."

I hang up. Leave your feelings at the door. Right.

If only it were that easy.

Today, your mission is to cheat on your spouse.

Today your mission is to fail a student.

Today your mission is to sleep with your direct supervisor.

Today your mission is to sleep with a student.

I read the mission text and gag.

"I'm not doing this," I say out loud.

"As an at will employee, you are welcome to quit at any time. You will, however, be required to return your headset and pay back any bonuses you've received since your onboarding. This includes recruitment bonuses."

"How much is that?" I ask Lia.

"Seven-thousand three-hundred and twenty-five dollars."

I look at the ballance in my account. $2,976.

"So somehow, I need to make up four grand?"

"Your current buyout is four-thousand three-hundred and forty-nine dollars. Would you like to terminate today?"

I shake my head.

"I can't."

"As an at will–"

"I get it. No. No I don't want to terminate."

"Recall that for each shift, you're compensated at a base rate of twenty-five dollars per hour."

"Fine," I snap.

I'll just run down the clock.

I wake up next to Sal. He makes me coffee. He asks what I'll be doing today.

"I'm not doing shit today."

What's your mission, I mean?

"I know. I'm not doing it. I'm supposed to sleep with a fucking student."

Well that sounds kind of hot.

"It's gross, Sal. My kids are fourteen. That's so messed up."

Don't you have a few upperclassmen?

"No. I'm the freshman art teacher. God. Some of them are thirteen, I think."

Well if it makes you feel better, they probably aren't really thirteen. You know–

"It doesn't."

Alright Bernie Sanders. Buck the system then. Good luck.

I can tell he's pissed.

"What do you mean?"

You'll see.

And I did. As soon as Sal left, I find out exactly what he means. There is… nothing at all to do.

I lay in bed.

"Lia, can I watch something?"

"Sure," the TV lights up.

"Frescetto Pizza, hot and fresh–"

"Lia, is this it?"

I already know the answer.

"These ads are targeted for your demographic breakdown. If you feel an ad is not appropriate for your demographic breakdown, say 'Curate my advertisements.'"

For thirty minutes, I watch ad after ad. Pizza, fast food, energy drinks, weight loss supplements, facial cleanser, yoga pants, sneakers… the list goes on and on. Finally, I can't take it anymore.

"Lia, turn the TV off."

The screen goes black.

"Lia, can I leave the house?"

"You may only leave the house in pursuit of your assigned mission. Would you like to go to work."

"No."

"Would you like to online shop?"

"No."

"Would you like to try a sample of–"

"No," I do not want to participate.

I do not want a $5 off coupon for the new Baja Chicken Taco. I do not want to try Chic Fil A's new extra spicy buffalo sauce. I do not want to smell or taste or feel or buy anything.

And so for three and a half hours, I simply sit, staring at the blank screen.

It's torture. The apartment is completely noiseless. The sun neither rises nor falls.

At one point, I feel myself, my real self, falling asleep.

A sharp electrical pulse runs down my spine. I yell.

"What was that?"

There is no lingering pain, but the sensation was enough to wake me immediately. I remember the time I accidentally carried my Corgi's electric collar across the underground fence. It felt just like that but in my head.

"When a player's biometrics indicate they've entered stage one of sleep, the player receives a harmless electrical shock of 45 volts."

"That fucking hurt."

"No sleeping on the job."

My ears prick up. And for the first time, I wonder if Lia is sentient. All this time, I've assumed she was a bot. She said she was a bot, didn't she?

"Fuck you, Lia," I say.

Another shock. This time longer.

"No sleeping on the job."

CHAPTER TWELVE

Don't Hate the Player

The second my headset comes off, I'm on the phone.

"Hi, you've reached the voicemail of Maya Evans. Please leave a message."

Fuck you, Maya.

I call the shelter. It's 10 p.m. But someone is always at the front desk, right?

"Agape Women's Shelter, this is the after hours emergency line. What's your emergency?"

"It's Alyssa. I'm a volunteer."

"Uhm, okay. Is this an emergency?"

I pause.

"Yes. Is Maya working?"

"No she's not. What's your emergency?"

Fuck. I hang up. What *is* my emergency?

I hit redial.

"Hi, you've reached—"

"Hey it's Alyssa, again. Sorry. I got disconnected. Maya accidentally left her phone at my place and it's been ringing off the hook. I think it's her daughter."

I hope and pray that Maya has a daughter. Or that if she doesn't, the girl on the other end doesn't know that.

"Uh, okay. I think Maya's at her other job tonight."

"Where is that?"

"You say her daughter called you?" she sounds confused.

I hesitate, "Yeah."

"I really don't think I should give out that information. Let me call Maya and see—"

"You can't though. Because I have her phone."

"Right. Well she works nights at the bar on Eastern. The White Rabbit."

"Great I'll bring it to her there."

Click.

I look up the location of the bar. It's a twenty five minute walk. Nope.

I call an Uber. Debbie will most certainly be having a word with me about this one. I just hope and pray the transaction isn't time stamped. "I was going to the bar to talk," isn't going to fly. That's the thing about being a liar—even your truths are suspect.

I've never been to The White Rabbit. I haven't been to any bars since the accident, actually. Under normal circumstances, I'd be paranoid. What if someone sees me? But my rage has made me single-minded. I need to talk to Maya. I don't even know what I'm going to say.

I'm just mad.

The bar is a total dive. It still smells like stale cigarette smoke, even though smoking indoors has been illegal for almost ten years. I smell whisky and light beer. And body—I smell sweat. It's a den of thieves, and I feel right at home.

My lizard brain wants to slump over the bar and forget why I came. That would be nice, actually.

Then I see Maya.

She's dressed in leggings and a black crop top. And she's wearing lipstick. She looks hot.

Maya sees me. She rolls her eyes. I wonder if the after hours girl called ahead. Probably.

"I hear my daughter needs me?" Maya sets a napkin down at the bar.

"I needed to know where you were. It was an emergency."

"I think we have different definitions of emergencies," sets an ice water in front of me. "You drinking?"

"No," I shake my head, "Maya this game is fucked up. You didn't tell me—"

"Hey," Maya leans in close, "We can't talk about this here. You crazy?"

"No one's listening. Besides," I say, "They're not going to remember this night anyway." Speaking from experience.

"Look," Maya sighs, "I get that you're upset. I understand that. But you can't go around ambushing people at work. I'm working, Alyssa. I'm not here to chat with customers."

"Well when is your break? I can wait."

"I'm not taking a break."

"Well I'm not leaving. You brought me into this, Maya," I lean in, "Me, and Grace and who the fuck knows who else."

"Grace," Maya shakes her head, "Grace isn't playing. And if she is, I didn't recruit her. That girl didn't speak two words to me the whole time she was staying. Who told you that?"

"Grace did," I say, "At the grocery store. She said she *had* to leave. Interpersonal conflicts."

"And so you assumed it was me," Maya's eyes narrow.

"Well you recruited me. And you didn't tell me *shit* about fucking a thirteen-year-old. That's so messed up."

I'm making a scene now. Maya looks around nervously.

"Fine," she takes her apron off.

We walk out the back, through the kitchen. I make a mental note to never order food from the Rabbit. Disgusting back there.

Outside Maya lights a cigarette. She takes a long drag.

"Alyssa, honey, this is a game. It's not real. So first off, you gotta keep telling yourself that."

"The world we're playing in isn't real," I agree, "But the people are. Their feelings are real."

"It's four hours of their lives. And then they can go back to whatever misery fills the rest of their week. Just like you and me."

"I don't think that makes it okay to–"

"What?"

"To do all this fucked up shit, Maya. The guy I'm married to said he *burnt* his wife. Like he fucking cooked her, man."

Maya laughs, "Yeah, but–"

"It's not funny," I say, "It's really sick. And people are watching us do it. Did you know that?"

"Of course I knew that. Alyssa, I have been playing for a long time. You think this is news to me?" She scoffs, "Honey I have news for *you*." She tosses the cigarette butt on the asphalt. "Whatever you've seen over these past few months ain't nothing. I've been playing for five years. You are not the first person I recruited, and you will not be the last. And, as a matter of fact, I *do* have a daughter. But when the on call girl told me you had my phone and 'my daughter' was calling? I laughed. You know why?"

"No," I shake my head. I can feel my stomach turning. I'm about to be caught in my lie.

"Because my daughter is laying in a hospital bed in my guest room. Hasn't used a phone in seven years. You know how much a caregiver costs, Alyssa?"

"No," God I feel like an idiot.

"Twenty-five an hour. Twenty-five an hour four days a week. That's $600 a week. And you know how she got there?"

"How?" I don't want to know. I feel sick.

"Drunk driver. On her way home from college. So. Let me ask you something, Alyssa."

I can feel my eyes welling with shame tears. I wish I hadn't come.

"Do me a favor right quick," she lights another cigarette, "Think back to when you spun for that first character. Do you remember that?"

"Yeah," I say.

"How many did you get?"

"Three I think."

"Did you use any?"

"I used one?"

"On what? Did you make yourself younger? Or did you make yourself a man?"

"I respun for–" I don't want to say. "I respun for my race."

Maya nods, "I bet you did. Who wouldn't? Who wouldn't want an edge? Yeah, I bet you did spin yourself a little lighter. And I don't blame you."

"I just don't want to play anymore."

"You don't want to play anymore?" Maya laughs, "What's your buyout?"

"Four grand."

"You got four grand squirreled away somewhere?"

"No," the tears are close now.

"You got some rich grandparents? A few heirlooms you could pawn."

"I'm not a thief, Maya."

"Oh please. You don't get to stop playing, Alyssa. Headset on or off. We are all playing The Game. We don't make the rules, but we are all playing The Game. The second you came into this world, you were playing. The second you had a dollar to your name, you were playing. The second you had a bank account, that's right–you were playing. You can't quit. Quitting just means you're losing. But so long as you live and breathe, honey, you're still playing The Game."

I wipe my nose with my sweatshirt.

Maya puts out her second cigarette on the brick wall. "Don't come by here again unless you want a drink."

And I'm alone in the dark once again.

CHAPTER THIRTEEN

Hate the Game

For six consecutive, mind-numbing shifts, I lay in bed. I refuse to taste samples of ravioli, refuse to engage in user research. I refuse to talk to Lia.

At the end of each shift, I withdraw $400—enough to eek by. Luckily, eeking is something I excel at.

Pasta is my friend. Pasta and peanut butter. Not together.

I consider the blood bank. I've never sold my blood before. Or my plasma. Whatever. Something about selling my own flesh, my own tissue, has always felt unsavory to me.

And it's not a donation. They sell it too. They mark it up and sell it. Your body.

But I've already sold my soul, so why not?

Sal knows I'm not participating.

Same mission?

He asks me over coffee (which I now refuse to drink).

I don't answer. And I don't return the question. Quite frankly, I'd rather not know.

I wonder when he's going to kill me. And I wonder how.

Eventually you're just going to have to bite the bullet.

He says it on his way out the door.

Bite the bullet. I learned the phrase in high school history. Before anesthesia, or when it wasn't available, soldiers were given a bullet to bite during especially painful procedures, amputations and the like.

I remember being amazed by the amount of pain a body can endure without dying.

That same fact terrifies me now.

I stave off the mission for as long as I can. I wonder if at some point, the system resets. A girl can dream. Just not in The Game.

Once or twice I fall asleep. I'm awoken by Lia each time.

"No sleeping in the game."

Our conversations are one-sided. *She knows,* I think to myself, *that it's only a matter of time before I have to complete this mission. She's smoking me out.*

And whether she knows or not, whether Lia is a sentient being on the other side of a black mirror or not, it's working.

Eventually, I cave. I have just under $300 in my account.

"Fine," I say, "Take me to work."

There is a special part of hell for people who use their power to sexually exploit others. The part of me that is Adrianna exists there now.

This particular shift ends at home. Sal is there, which is unusual.

As he opens the door to our home, a seventeen-year-old slides past him.

"I'm, uh, just here for tutoring," she says.

Sal locks the door behind him.

So you finally got off your high horse.

"That horse is dead."

Look, we all go through this phase. But you had to do it, Adrianna. This is your job.

"Yeah, okay."

Good people do bad things, Adrianna. Most people just don't get caught. And the ones that do are crucified.

My heart drops. Where have I heard that before. I can feel my pulse quickening.

"Darren?"

Click.

***

I set the headset on the table.

My breath is hard and fast.

I dial Darren's number.

No answer.

Again. Again. Again.

I don't leave a voicemail. Why bother? I know where he lives.

What if it wasn't him? What if that was a line from a movie I don't know?

I google the line on the Uber ride to his apartment. Nothing. But what are the chances? What are the chances that in a game with thousands and thousands of people, I'm married to one of the seven people I know.

I nearly trip up the stairs. I can't remember his apartment number. There are six units in the building. But we went up three flights of stairs.

I press six.

"Hey," a female voice sounds through the intercom.

"Hi," I choose my words carefully, "Is this Darren's place?"

"No, this is Kirsten. Darren is next door. Number six."

"Thanks," I answer. Easy enough. Too easy. She must assume I know him. And I do. But still.

I press six.

"Hi," Darren's voice this time.

"It's Alyssa."

Click.

I'm in.

I jog up the stairs. The door is already open.

"Is it Alyssa, or Adrianna?" Darren asks. He's sitting on the couch. A half empty bottle of Jim Beam is open on the coffee table.

"I thought you were sober?"

"I am," he laughs.

"What are the chances?" I ask.

"So slim it's worth drinking to," he pours me a glass. "Cheers."

I take a sip. It burns like communion wine. I shiver.

Darren laughs, "May it wash away your sins." He's drunk. I can tell. It's only been an hour since our shift ended but he's absolutely gone.

"So what do we do?" I ask.

"About what?"

"About The Game. Do we disclose?"

"Absolutely not. You remember that apartment you had when you started playing?"

"Yeah."

"When you disclose, you start over."

"But you still get whatever's in your account, right?"

Darren laughs. He takes a long drink. "Nope. And I learned that the hard way. Fucking bitch."

I raise my eyebrows.

"Not you. The first girl."

"The one you burnt?"

"The one before that," another drink. "It's a dog eat dog world."

More like rat eat rat.

"So we don't disclose? What if they find out? I said your name."

"Just say you were confused. They aren't *always* watching."

I nod.

I need to get out of here. But first, "Darren, do you remember Grace?"

Darren scratches his head. He's swimming, head slowly bobbing from left to right.

"Grace…" he repeats, like a zombie.

"Yes, Grace. Room two. She was tiny, really tiny. She left like a few months ago."

He considers it. "Oh, Grace? Grace DeVries?"

I have no idea, "Sure."

He scoffs, "That bitch said I came on to her."

"Did you?"

"No. No way. If anything, she came on to me." He looks at his empty glass, then reaches for the bottle.

I wish I could say I haven't been there. But I have. At a certain point, the glass seems almost excessive. Why measure? Why count.

"You slept with Grace?" I ask.

"She was basically begging me, Alyssa."

A small trickle of caramel whiskey runs down the corner of his mouth and onto his shirt. The charm is gone. He bobs like a small boat in a dark ocean, barely floating, barely above the water, sinking fast. Soon he'll be gone. Soon the blackness will consume him.

I feel sad. For him. For me. For Grace. For Maya. For Maya's daughter. And I wonder which is easier to bear, the dark emptiness of the water or the biting chill of the air.

For so much of my life, I've chosen the water. The nothingness of the water, the water that cradles and supports, that fills your lungs and rots your gut—that water is my home.

"You should probably go," he says.

I nod, "Yeah, okay."

He lays on the couch while I put my coat on, look for my phone, my keys.

I'm halfway out the door before—

"Hey Alyssa?"

"Yeah," I turn around, hoping he'll save me.

"Promise you won't disclose, okay?"

"I promise," I close the door behind me.

***

G-r-a-c-e D-e-v-r-i-e-s

I type it into my phone.

It's a strange last name. How many could there be?

As it turns out, a lot.

I open Facebook.

G-r-a-c-e D-e-v-r-i-e-s

She definitely lives here. But what if she moved? Or what if she uses her maiden name on Facebook? What if DeVries *is* her maiden name?

I open profile after profile after profile.

Then finally, I find her. Grace Anneka DeVries (Tyler). Her profile picture is her and two blonde kids picking apples. They're little. One looks two and the other one is Garret's age.

It's the type of photo me and Molly would make fun of. I realize Grace is my age. She seemed so much older. She's thirty-one.

She looks healthy. She looks like she's not limping, at least.

I breathe a sigh of relief.

Add friend. I send the request. Not that she'll want to be my friend—she made that pretty clear in the grocery store.

But there's no harm in trying.

Within minutes, I receive a notification.

Grace Anneka Devries (Tyler) has accepted your friend request.

I'm surprised. But maybe she needs help. Or maybe she can't remember who I am.

I open her profile. Hundreds of cutesy mommy pictures. I'm looking for the husband, the partner, the one responsible for the limp. Nowhere to be found. Maybe he's out of the picture. Maybe she didn't go back. Maybe the guy at the corner store was someone new.

Maybe she did what any sensible girl would do and deleted all his pictures the second she got to Agape.

I smile. Maybe Grace is okay.

I make a mental note to apologize to Maya. It won't mean much now but–

I stop scrolling. A comment on a post from three days ago:

Channel Richards
We miss you Gracie grl. So much light and love. Rest in peace, angel

No.

I scroll down.

Ryan Winn
No words can explain how sad, angry and lost I feel for all victims of domestic abuse and violence. YOU ARE NOT ALONE. RIP Grace. We miss you

No. No. No.

Sharon Devries
My gorgeous daughter. Not a day goes by that I don't think of you. your boys cry for you every day. It feels like the world has stopped. I trust you're in better hands now and smiling down on us each day. I love you, gracie xoxo mom

It's moments like these that the water calls for me. I want to disappear beneath its surface. I want to melt into nothing.

If I had anything to drink, I would. But I don't.

So for the first time, I sit still while the storm rages around me, floating on the raft that is my breath. One breath at a time.

In to the count of four. Hold at the top.

The rain is angry and cold. It stings my skin and soaks my clothes.

Out to the count of six. Hold at the bottom.

But in spite of it all, I float. My head stays above water. My raft holds. And eventually, the storm passes, and I'm still alive.

CHAPTER FOURTEEN

Reincarnation

"Good afternoon, Alyssa," Lia greets me.

I say nothing.

Lia analyzes my biometrics. Normal, other than my heart rate which is a little high.

"Do you have anything to disclose?" Lia asks.

I pause. What happens if I do and Darren doesn't?

Does he even remember my promise? And why did I promise him that? I don't owe him anything.

"Alyssa, do you have anything to disclose?"

"No," I say finally, though I'm not entirely sure why. I have nothing to lose.

A long pause.

"Unfortunately Alyssa, another player has disclosed a relationship with you outside the game. This disclosure, in combination with your biometrics, suggests dishonesty on your part."

I'm waiting for the shock. *No lying in The Game.*

"Your partner has been given the opportunity to end your relationship and has chosen to do so. You may now begin your shift."

That's it? No electrocution? "So, I'm not fired?"

"No. However in the future, it is in your best interest to disclose if your identity has been compromised."

"Okay," I'm suspicious. "So can I see my mission?"

"You have no mission today," Lia says coldly, even for her.

My austere apartment fades into view. The twin bed, the nightstand, my little lamp–all untouched.

The only difference is–

"Lia, I smell smoke."

END OF BOOK ONE

AUTHOR'S NOTE

Dear Reader,

Thank you so much for taking the time to read my work. I consider it a work in progress and am happy to hear your feedback.

Please consider reviewing this book on goodreads.com.

If you'd like to start a conversation, I'm reachable via Instagram. My handle is @alexandra_bos.

I hope to hear from you.

-Alex

Made in the USA
Monee, IL
13 July 2023